Dawn of the the Living-Impaired

and Other Messed Up Zombie Stories

Christine Morgan

Copyright © 2019 by Christine Morgan.

ISBN: 9781639510641

Published by Death's Head Press, an imprint of Dead Sky Publishing, LLC Miami Beach, Florida

www.deadskypublishing.com

Cover and Interior artwork by Justin T. Coons

Dawn of the Living-Impaired (*The Book of All Flesh* 2002 / *Best of All Flesh* 2009)

Seven Brains, Ten Minutes (*The Book of Final Flesh* 2003 / *Z: Zombie Stories* 2011)

The Barrow-Maid (*History is Dead* 2007 / *Z: Zombie Stories* 2011)

Cured Meat (*The World is Dead* 2009)

Family Life (*Rom Zom* 2014)

A Tower to the Sky (*Tales of the Undead: Undead in Pictures* 2014)

Good Boy (*Zombiefied Reloaded* 2014)

Thought He Was A Goner (*Legacy of the Reanimator* 2015)

Contents

DAWN OF THE LIVING-IMPAIRED

"WELCOME BACK TO *DAYBREAK Coast to Coast*, with your host, Elaine Kristin," the pre-recorded announcer voice-over said.

Elaine turned her megawatt smile into Camera 1, her impeccably-coiffed caramel locks falling perfectly over the shoulders of her rich turquoise blouse.

"In just a while, we'll be joining our Home Styles Consultant, Frances Meade, who'll be showing us how you can decorate your entire house for the holidays with the contents of your recycling bins! But first, in our continuing effort to keep you up-to-date on events here and around the world, we have two special guests with us to discuss perhaps the most controversial issue of our time."

She shifted her gaze to Camera 2, knowing that an inset screen would now be showing scenes from some of the choicer news segments and home video clips. But nothing *too* icky, of course, nothing to put the millions of consumers off their breakfast. The sponsors wouldn't appreciate that, since many of them hawked cereal, orange juice, and coffee, along with the usual run of ads for household cleansers and feminine hygiene products.

So instead of the famous, grisly footage of what had happened at last month's Entertainment Achievement Awards (for once, Elaine was glad instead of incensed that she hadn't been nominated), they ran the ones of the disinterred milling aimlessly outside of a closed shopping mall like impatient shoppers before a big sale.

"Since the first of them rose and walked away from their mortuary slabs and caskets six months ago," Elaine went on, ignoring the small sound of pained disapproval from her left, "their numbers have increased drastically, in a wide-sweeping epidemic that has affected nearly every nation. Each government has taken their own steps to combat what is seen as both a menace and health risk. Their solutions have primarily taken the form of military action, eradication, and disposal."

Camera 1 panned back to include Elaine, her comfy dove-colored chair, the cozy conversational set, and the fake windows that looked out on a photo mural of a sunswept, smog-free cityscape. It was no place that could ever be seen in reality, consisting as it did of computer-melded snippets of New York, Los Angeles, Seattle, and Chicago.

"Here in America, the land of the free," Elaine said, "the efforts of the military have run into a roadblock. I'm speaking of the so-called 'zombie rights movement,' and with me today are General Jason Gillespie, head of the U.S. task force organized to deal with the situation ..."

Gillespie, sitting to her right, nodded brusquely into the camera. His steel-grey hair was cropped close, his dark eyes both hooded and piercing. A sort of stern charisma, all iron and resolve, radiated from him. He wouldn't have been photogenic enough to run for office, even without the knotted white scar that scrawled from his eye to his chin, but in his crisp uniform and with his jaw firmly set, he was a striking figure.

"Good morning, Elaine," he said, with a voice both deep and harsh, the sort of voice that belonged shouting orders from the top of a trench while bullets stitched the air.

"... and Doctor Karen Wyatt-Anderson, noted psychiatrist and president of NALI." Elaine shifted her position to face the other woman. "Doctor Wyatt-Anderson, can you tell us a little about your organization?"

Karen Wyatt-Anderson was a cool blonde in a severe suit, navy blue skirt and blazer over a cream silk blouse. Her features were aristocratic and patrician. Her spine was even more rigid, her shoulders more stiffly held, than even the general. When she met Elaine's gaze, her eyes were winter-blue and about as chilling.

"Yes, Elaine," she said. "To begin, I must object to your use of the term 'zombie rights.'

NALI stands for the National Alliance for the Living-Impaired, and we are dedicated to correcting the damaging misconceptions revolving around our clients."

"They *are* zombies," rumbled Gillespie.

"That's like calling those with a mental illness 'nuts,'" Wyatt-Anderson countered sharply. "It is a hurtful term. NALI would like to see it stricken from popular usage. Along with several others."

"What others?" Elaine asked politely, much too good at this to let herself smirk.

"The frequent derogatory or belittling phrases involving the word 'dead,'" the doctor replied. "Whenever someone refers to someone else as 'dead meat,' or claims to be 'dead on their feet,' it reflects poorly on our clients."

"Your clients dig themselves out of their graves and eat people," Gillespie pointed out.

"It's a contagion, it's spreading, and it needs to be dealt with. Decisively, and soon. It's unclean."

"That's the very attitude NALI is seeking to change." Wyatt-Anderson returned her attention to Elaine, seeking sympathy. "Elaine, these people - yes, *people* - are our friends and neighbors, our families. They deserve to be treated with the dignity and respect they had in life. They should not be feared, reviled, or hunted down."

"But haven't they changed, doctor?" Elaine said. "They're not the same."

"They're not the same as they were, no. But neither is someone who has suffered a debilitating brain injury, or fallen into a coma, or been stricken with a mental illness or decline in cognition. Yet, in those cases, those people are still cared for. Their basic needs are still met."

"Basic needs!" The general leaned forward. "Lady, the only basic need a zombie's got is to chow down on human flesh! I've *seen* these things in action. I was in New York during the big July breakout. I saw one bunch of them overturn a busload of kids and dig right in!"

"And how did you handle the July breakout?" Wyatt-Anderson shot back. "By gunning down thousands of the living-impaired, in direct violation of their civil rights!"

"Damn straight! They're not people anymore! They're corpses. Their civil rights went out the window the minute they pulled themselves out of the ground and started helping themselves to brain take-out!"

Elaine knew there was a time to intervene and a time to sit back and let the interviews take their course. This was the latter. She discreetly picked up her coffee cup (emblazoned with the sponsor's logo, naturally), and sipped as the studio audience enjoyed the argument.

"It has been consistently proven that the living-impaired retain rudimentary memories of their past lives and habits. They are able to recognize familiar faces --"

"And bite 'em off to get at the gooey bits," snarled Gillespie. "They need to be wiped out."

"Destroying them is not the answer!"

"What is? We could have had this country cleansed by now, if you people hadn't come along whining about tolerance. What would you rather do? Get 'em all in a circle, hold hands, sing 'Kumbaya'?"

"With proper treatment, the living-impaired can be brought to a reasonable level of functioning."

"What sort of treatment?" Elaine interjected smoothly.

"Primarily therapy and medication --"

"God bless America," the general muttered as a curse, rolling his eyes. "On the couch, Mr. Bodybag, tell me about your mother."

Doctor Wyatt-Anderson archly ignored him and went on speaking to Elaine, who was nodding encouragingly. "Their desire for flesh, which is simply another form of addiction, can be treated with a patch."

"A patch?" Elaine urged.

"The Necroderm C-Q," she explained. "It is a time-release appetite suppressant, combined with a craving inhibitor."

"Does it come in a gum?" Gillespie asked snidely.

"No," Wyatt-Anderson said, "but there is a liquid form which can be injected in stronger doses. We use that to stabilize clients in crisis."

"Suppose that you can control their addiction," Elaine said. "What then?"

"Then we enroll them in a series of programs. Anger management. Coping skills. Job training. We help them and encourage them to manage their symptoms and compensate for their condition, with the goal of being able to exist in a non-restrictive environment."

"Non-restrictive ... you mean on their own?"

"Yes, Elaine, but that's a slow and tedious process. At the moment, we have over six hundred of the living-impaired placed in residential facilities, and thousands more in more intensive hospital-style settings. But millions more are out there, desperately in need of our services. The hardest part of our job is outreach, getting help to these people. Thanks to the efforts of those like the general here, most of the living-impaired are too afraid to come forward."

"Recent statistics have shown that the living-impaired population has outnumbered the homeless and the mentally ill," Elaine said. "When even those people couldn't receive adequate help, can NALI realistically offer their services to everyone?"

"Sadly, Elaine, we can't. NALI just doesn't have the staff or resources to extend all the help we'd like. Funding for our programs is practically nonexistent, depending almost entirely on private donations from families who have been touched by this tragedy. But you mentioned the homeless and the mentally ill ... the living-impaired population hasn't so much outnumbered them, as it has absorbed them."

"Yeah, they feed on the ones they can catch," Gillespie said. "The bums, street people, winos, loonies. If they leave enough meat on the bones, those ones get up and start walking, too."

The doctor swept him with a scathing look. "With the drastic decline in those populations, one would expect that there would be considerable funding left over. Money that had been going toward mental health and housing rehab programs could, and *should,* be funneled into ours. Yet that's not happening, Elaine, and it needs to be."

"What about the Center for Disease Control?" Elaine asked. "What's their stance? I had heard that this was being treated as a communicable disease ... postmortem infectious necrivorism, I believe was the term. Lots of people are concerned about how to keep themselves safe."

Gillespie nodded. "One bite, and they've got you. Nothing you can do. Even a little bite. If it breaks the skin, you're a goner. First it kills you, and then it brings you back. I saw a man get bit on the finger, hardly more than a scratch. But the next day, he was dead, and the day after that, we had to put a gun to his forehead and shower his brains all over the wall."

"The key to containing the spread of the illness is to avoid exposure," Wyatt-Anderson said. "The use of universal precautions, to prevent the introduction of the infected material-"

"Zombie spit," interjected the general, lifting his lip in a sneer. "Thing to do is eliminate the *source*. If there were no goddamn zombies, no one would have to worry about catching it. We find them, shoot them, burn what's left, and there you go. End of story, end of danger."

"Is that how you'd propose to handle other contagious illnesses, General?" Wyatt-Anderson asked accusingly. "AIDS, hepatitis, TB? This isn't the Dark Ages, and we will not treat patients like condemned criminals! They are victims of a terrible, terrible disease. We owe it to them to help, not draw plague circles around them!"

Elaine, responding to increasingly urgent signaling from her producer, cut in with another of her brilliant smiles. "We have to take a short break for some important messages, but we'll be back with General Gillespie and Doctor Wyatt-Anderson in a few minutes to take questions from our studio audience. And we'll also meet Barb and Danny, two of NALI's success stories."

The sign switched from ON AIR to OFF, and canned elevator music issued from the speakers over the audience. A couple of crew members came onstage to check and fiddle with this and that, and Elaine motioned for a refill on coffee.

"You're bringing some of those *things* out here?" asked Gillespie, with barely-contained rage. His face had reddened, making the pale scar stand out in vivid relief.

"Don't be afraid, General," Wyatt-Anderson said condescendingly. "The counselors have everything under control."

"How *do* you keep them under control?" Elaine asked. "It's fine and well to talk about universal precautions and not getting bit, but when you're dealing with a new zom ... a new client, how do you even get close enough to slap the patches on them?"

"Some direct methods are necessary," the doctor admitted. "They can be stunned or subdued by an electrical charge. Before the effects wear off, we get them under restraints to begin treatment."

"Waste of time," growled Gillespie. "Waste of money. You think you're going to rehabilitate zombies, put them back in regular society? That's crazy, that's all it is. Crazy."

"Thirty seconds," warned one of the production assistants.

Elaine thanked him with a nod, and got up. She smoothed her skirt - white, with a tropical floral pattern in shades of turquoise - and took the handheld microphone.

"And ... we're live in three, two, one!"

"Welcome back," Elaine said brightly. "We've been listening to some rather opposing viewpoints on today's topic. Doctor Wyatt-Anderson, president of NALI, supports compassionate caregiving and treatment for the living-impaired. General Gillespie feels that zombies are a threat and must be handled with extreme prejudice. Now, let's see what our audience thinks."

She held out the microphone to a clean-cut young college boy in a cableknit sweater. He stammered into it, flustered by the proximity of the camera, and then recovered.

"Hi, Elaine, hi. My question is for the doctor. Do you, personally, work with the zombies? Er ... with the living-impaired?"

Wyatt-Anderson gave him a cool, lofty look. "In my capacity with NALI, I work very closely with the staff of several hospitals and facilities. My main function is in training and education."

"So that's a no?" he pressed. "You don't work personally, hands-on, with the stiffs? You don't have to look at them, smell them, worry that they might take a chunk out of you?"

"I have seen several living-impaired clients," she said curtly.

The college guy looked straight into the camera and hoisted one eyebrow knowingly.

Elaine thanked him and moved on to a portly man possessing the bulldog jowls and the sorrowful eyes of a basset hound.

"Albert Lawry, here," he said, gaze fixed on the microphone. "I just ... my wife, Helen ... she died a year ago ... I was wondering, doctor, if you could help me find her? She was buried in

Oregon, with her parents, and when everything started I went to the cemetery, but she wasn't there. Do you have a list or something?"

"I'm sorry, Mr. Lawry ... most of the time, our clients have no identification. We try to track down their records, but it's a slow process. If you call NALI, at 1-888-555-3323 --"

"That's 555-DEAD," the college student announced quickly, drawing a laugh from the audience and a flush of chagrined realization from the doctor.

She regained her composure, but if telepathy were real and could kill, there'd be one attractive twenty-something laid out on the floor. "If you call NALI and leave your name and information, we can contact you should we locate your wife."

Elaine moved to the next waving hand, which belonged to a teenage girl with intricately beaded and cornrowed hair. "General Gillespie, my dad is in the Marines, and he says that zombies can only be killed if you blow their heads off. Is that true, or can you burn them?"

"I hardly think that's an appropriate question!" Doctor Wyatt-Anderson said.

"It's a good question." The general faced the girl. "As near as the scientists have been able to tell, the only way to stop them is to take out the brain. Fire might do it, eventually, but in the meantime, they'd still be running around. And I'll tell you one thing ... it may be hard to believe, but a burnt zombie stinks worse than a regular one."

Karen Wyatt-Anderson's lips had drawn together in a line so thin and tight that they'd almost disappeared. "I must once again object to your choice of language! These are people we're talking about. Wives, husbands, sons, daughters, mothers, and fathers! You demean and degrade them by referring to them in those terms!"

A thin, intense woman with long dark hair popped up beside Elaine. "They're *dead!* Can't you get that through your politically-correct skull?"

"They've come back. Not all the way, granted, but they've made the effort."

"Effort! Some alien germ or solar radiation made corpses walk, that's all it was! Not God, not their own free will! Who would want to come back as something like that? Who'd want to live like that? I say that putting them out of their misery would be doing them a favor, not sending them to some twelve-step program!"

Savage applause, not the least of which was from the general, greeted the intense woman's remarks. Mixed in were cries of "You said it!" and "All right!" and one man chanting,

"Bring out your dead! Bring out your dead!"

"Why don't we?" chirped Elaine, in her most vivacious talk-show-hostess tone. "Let's bring out Barb and Danny, and hear what they have to say!"

The college boy and the man who'd been chanting both cupped their hands around their mouths to make megaphones and called, "Braaaaaaaiiiiiiinns!" in slow, dragging imitation of the undead.

The good doctor stood up. "I will not have them subjected to this blatantly hostile abuse! NALI's purpose is to increase public awareness and help our clients."

"Maybe it would help for everyone to see the progress they've made under treatment," Elaine suggested. "We're all operating on the basis of what we've seen in the media, and probably have a negative, sensationalized view."

"Progress!" Gillespie snorted. "Couple of zombies, hosed off and put in clean clothes. Maybe you can train 'em like animals, but they're still flesh-eating monsters. Suppose you bring them out here and they decide it's an all-you-can-eat buffet?"

"Barb has been flesh-free for eight weeks," Wyatt-Anderson said huffily. "Danny, for almost as long. They're proof that the patch and the treatment are effective, two of our most compensated clients."

Elaine caught the eye of one of the backstage crew, and he responded with a nod. Moments later, a small group emerged from the side door of the set. Three men and a woman, all in pristine white lab coats, ushered in two shuffling figures. An appalled, fascinated "Ooooh!" came from the audience, accompanied by a shifting rustle as they all leaned forward to get a good look. For most of them, this was the first time they'd seen one of the unfortunate necrivores, except on television.

The larger of the two, introduced as Barb, must have been a huge woman in life and hadn't diminished much since. A drab mustard-colored sweatsuit neither concealed nor flattered the drooping swell of her belly, or the pendulous melon-sized breasts that bobbled like loosely-filled sacks of gelatin. Her behind was truly mythic in its proportions, and with her head bent down against the glare of the studio lighting, her chins descended to her chest in a series of mushy folds. They'd obviously made an effort to get her presentable. Her skin was doughy and blue-grey, but she was clean and not visibly maggot-ridden. What was left of her hair, clumps of mahogany brown that might have otherwise been pretty, had been drawn neatly back in a scrunchied ponytail. She had the sadly sweet face of so many hopelessly obese women, hinting at the beauty that might have been hers, had her life taken a different turn.

Danny moved with considerably more ease, as it would have taken about eight of him to make up one Barb. He couldn't have been more than ten years old when he died, and the evidence of his death was present in the form of bite marks and missing hunks of flesh up and down his scrawny arms, as well as a malformed dent in the side of his head. The ghost of an impish smile lurked around his slack, dry lips. He wore jeans, an oversized football jersey, and high-top sneakers, like any other kid. Yards of spice-scented wrappings might have suited him better, for he appeared wizened and dry, more mummified than rotting. His dark skin had taken on a hue and texture reminiscent of ash-coated beef jerky.

General Gillespie made a sound somewhere between a moan and a snarl as the two zombies shambled closer. Their attendants stopped them at the center of the stage, Cameras 1 and 2 zooming in for close-ups. Both of their patches were in plain sight, pasted to the sides of their necks just below the ear (or, in Danny's case, the crushed and mangled cartilage that used to be an ear). In a final bizarre touch, the patches were, for some reason, the gleaming plastic pink-tan that used to be called 'flesh' by the crayon people, a color that didn't even match the skin of any race of the living. On Barb and Danny, it was as hectic as a clown's vivid red cheeks.

Doctor Wyatt-Anderson crossed her arms smugly beneath her breasts and threw Gillespie a silent "Told you so!" as the nervous tittering and revolted gasps of the audience gave way to murmurings of pity. Elaine understood their feelings, for there was something unspeakably tragic and solemn about the pair. They stood, slouched by both the poor posture of death and the inescapable defeated hopelessness of their circumstances.

Danny goggled at the nearest camera. One of his eyes was milky but otherwise normal; the other was distended from the socket as if it had been popped out and replaced, but the fit would never quite be the same. That orb was roadmapped with broken veins, and a purpled corona engulfed the pupil.

The bleak incomprehension in their stares changed as they took in the sight of the studio audience, dozens and dozens of healthy humans. The glint put Elaine in mind of reluctant dieters confronted with a bakery window.

What must they look like to those glassy gazes? A parade of meaty limbs and delectable torsos? Didn't they always say that you couldn't help someone who didn't want to be helped? What was the treatment doing to them? As far as she knew, as far as anyone knew, the living dead came back with only one driving impulse. To eat. And now that had been taken away from them. What did that leave?

"My God," Elaine heard herself say. "This is terrible!"

"The growth rate of the living-impaired population," Wyatt-Anderson said, "has leveled off, thanks to the increase in cremation as a form of funerary services. But there are still millions of them out there, and they need your help."

Gillespie shook his head. "What they need is to be sent back where they came from. That one lady was right. This is no way to be!"

Barb swiveled slowly in his direction. Watching her move was like watching the gaseous atmosphere of Jupiter rotate, bands of flesh shifting and sliding at different rates. A whiff of her odor reached Elaine. Mostly soap and talcum powder, but underneath was a faintly rancid, wholly repugnant reek of spoilage.

The general realized with utter horror that he was the focus of three-hundred-plus pounds of zombie attention, and took an involuntary step back.

"Deaaad," Barb said, forcing the word sluggishly through liquefying vocal cords.

"Dead," Danny seconded, his voice more clear, but raspy as a file on sandpaper.

"And they should stay that way," said someone from the audience. Elaine recognized the intense brunette without needing to look. "Dead things should stay that way. This is wrong, can't you see it, wrong!"

Doctor Wyatt-Anderson stepped forward to argue, but Barb's chins tripled and receded as she nodded. "Rrrr-rrronnng!" Her pudgy, sausage-fingered hand floated up as if tied to a helium balloon. It wandered aimlessly around her head for a moment, pulled strands of hair from the scrunchie to hang lank in her face, and then found the edge of the patch. Two of her fingernails peeled loose as she dug at it.

"Barb, stop it," said one of the attendants.

Danny squinted up at his behemothic companion, some dim understanding welling in his muddy eyes.

Barb's patch came unstuck with a grisly squelching noise, tearing away a spongy mat of skin and flesh with it. "Dead!" she shrieked. "Dead-dead-dead!"

The attendants rushed in, bringing heavy-duty tasers out of concealed holsters. Elaine, rooted to the spot, was buffeted as the audience yielded to instinct and thundered for the exits.

"Dead-dead-dead!" Danny parroted, and ripped the patch from his own neck so vigorously that he nearly beheaded himself. The ivory knobs of his vertebrae poked through like stepping stones.

"Stop her!" Wyatt-Anderson ordered above the din. Then, incredibly, "We'll never get funding like this!"

It was, Elaine would later think, a pretty crappy set of last words. Barb lumbered forward with the force of a charging rhino, and crushed the doctor's ribcage with one swing of her massive arm.

Still unable to move, hypnotized by the spectacle, Elaine observed with detached marvel the way the impact sent ripples through the zombie's flab.

Barb seized Wyatt-Anderson, pulled her close as if going for a kiss, and clamped her jaws on the doctor's shoulder. Elaine, in a space beyond horror now, batted at Barb's face with the microphone and squashed her nose into a soggy ruin. Barb let go of her victim.

An attendant grabbed for Danny as Doctor Wyatt-Anderson's body was hitting the ground. The dead child writhed, snake-fast, and got a mouthful of muscle, eliciting a scream that was more terror than pain ... and it was a lot of pain.

Barb, stepping mostly over but partly on the fallen psychiatrist and, cracking bones like twigs underfoot, reached for the darling of the daytime talk shows. Elaine thrust out the microphone and Barb chomped into it, masticating furiously on the spongy black covering before spitting it aside.

Someone dropped an iron safe onto a solid hardwood floor. Or at least that was what Elaine's first thought was as the colossal boom resonated through the studio. It wasn't until the side of Barb's skull blossomed out in a pulpy yellow and grey spray that she realized what had happened. The giant body went down so hard that it wouldn't have been surprising to hear car alarms go off in the parking lot outside. Elaine very nearly went down with it, as Barb's flailing hand snared the front of her blouse. She was yanked backward to safety by the college guy in the cableknit sweater.

General Gillespie, his uniform jacket all askew and a holster visible tucked into the rear of his pants, leveled a gun roughly the size of a small cannon at the attendants struggling with Danny. Electricity leapt and sizzled as they tried to use their tasers to subdue the ravenous boy, but Danny was having none of it. The taste of hot blood and warm meat was in his mouth for the first time in weeks, and he was not going to be denied.

"Get clear!" ordered the general. When they didn't obey, he strode into their midst, flinging them aside like dolls.

Danny was atop the bitten attendant, whose thrashings had ceased once zombie teeth tore open his throat. The dead boy had burrowed his face under the attendant's chin and was snacking and slurping loudly.

Gillespie slammed his foot down on Danny's back, set the barrel of the gun to his head, and with a wincing grimace that reminded Elaine of the way her mom would look when fishing around in a turkey for the giblet packet, pulled the trigger. That safe hit the floor again. The bullet plowed through Danny's small and already cracked skull, out the other side, and lodged somewhere in the attendant.

Panic and chaos ensued. The exits were crammed with desperately shoving people, and one of the other attendants, in a total loss of sanity, tried to tase the general, but Gillespie had the presence of mind to drop his gun and disarm the man hand-to-hand rather than blow away a living human on live TV.

Speaking of which ... Elaine saw that, while the cameramen had fled, the lights and the 'ON AIR' sign were still on. Camera

1 had been knocked aslant and was getting nothing but stampeding, fleeing feet. But Camera 2 was getting everything.

"It's all right!" General Gillespie bellowed. "They're down! Both down!"

His words took the edge off of the furor, but it all went to hell again a split second later.

With a sudden convulsive lurch, Doctor Wyatt-Anderson pushed herself upright. She held herself awkwardly, with half of her ribs caved in, and one arm dangled crazy-jointed and limp. The general, the college guy, and Elaine together shouted a word that would have been edited out or bleeped on tape, but they were still live, still rolling.

Wyatt-Anderson's gaze fell upon them. Formerly haughty and cold, it was now filled with a mindless hunger. Her lips drew back to expose a view that would have been right at home in a toothpaste commercial. She darted forward and swiped a handful of manicure at Gillespie.

The gun roared again, the shot hitting Wyatt-Anderson in the temple and smashing most of the top of her head off. She cartwheeled in a tumble over the dove-grey chair that Elaine vowed never to sit in again, and came to rest in a heap at the bottom of the window with its fake cityscape scene.

Elaine looked, wide-eyed, and saw the intense dark-haired woman lower the general's gun.

"Wow," said the college guy shakily. "I guess she wasn't just president of the National Alliance for the Living-Impaired --"

It was either the hellish insanity of the moment, or the reek of blood and decomposition, making them take leave of their senses, but the rest of them came in with him on the end.

"She's also a client!" they chorused, and finally someone in the control room had the good sense to go to commercial.

SEVEN BRAINS, TEN MINUTES

THE BRAIN LAY IN front of me, pink-grey and pulsing in the sun.

I could see the edge of skull, sheared off so neatly by the cranial saw. The bony rim of nature's bowl. With its contents bulging up out of it like an extra-large scoop of ice cream. Or maybe gelatin. Hadn't they even, in the dim and gone days before the world ended, made gelatin molds shaped like brains?

If I pretended that's what this was ...

No. It might quiver, it might shimmer, it might have the same gelatinous quality, but I knew better. I knew that the temperature would be all wrong. Warm. Body temperature, it'd be.

Of course it would. And why not? The body was still alive.

The guy it belonged to was in shock. He'd be dead – and probably glad of it – within minutes. Sooner, if I did what I was up here to do. What I had to do.

I couldn't.

Not even for Val.

Did she even know? Did she even recognize me? Or had fear taken her beyond all that?

The sun beat down. A rusty haze of dust filled the air. I could hear the flap of canvas and the sounds of the crowd. I could hear the Fat Man's laughter from above and behind me.

That was where Val would be. Up there in the bed of the customized pick-up truck. With the Fat Man. Naked. Chained. A blue ribbon wrapped around her waist.

The others in the line to either side of me were straining against the iron bar, teeth bared, foamy drool on what was left of their lips. We had our hands tied behind us and numbers on placards strung on ropes around our necks.

The bell rang.

The bar dropped.

"And theeeeeyyyyyy're off!" the Fat Man bellowed.

We picked up Patty just outside of Bakersfield.

I didn't want to. I would have roared on past and left her in a whirl of grit and soot.

But when Patty waved, Jess said we should stop.

"We can't take care of everybody," I said. "We've got to look out for ourselves."

"Don't be a jerk, Scotty," Val said. "Stop the car."

"Don't call me Scotty. You know I hate it."

"Scotty, Scotty, Scotty," she sneered.

The end of the world hadn't done a thing to her looks or her attitude. It hadn't put a shake in her hands or purple circles under her eyes or anything.

Gorgeous.

But a bitch.

"I think we should stop," Rick said, checking out the thin blonde. He was Val's brother, but didn't have any of her good looks. Skinny, pimply, a loser from the word 'go.'

Two of a kind, that was me and Rick.

"We are a girl short," Jess said, putting his arm around Sharon. She only rocked in her seat and hugged the dog. "Us, you and Val, and poor Rick left over."

"Oh, puh-lease." Val's laugh was a snort. "Me and Scotty? Don't make me sick."

I hated her.

I wanted her so much it burned.

When everything started, with the deadies and all, Rick and I were the first ones to figure out what would happen, how it would all go down. We read comic books and horror novels and watched all those old movies. We knew.

Everyone else went around in denial. First, they said it was nothing but rumors, urban legends, hoaxes. Then, when it was proved real, they said it would blow over. Then, that the government would take care of it. Then, that scientists would find a cure. *Then* ...

And by *then*, well, there wasn't much of anyone left who wasn't taking bites out of people.

The crowd roared. Deadies lunged, with jaws gaping and putrescent tongues snaking out. They went face-first into the opened domes of the skulls and commenced a smacking, slurping, munching feast.

I shook so hard my teeth clattered. Someone threw a crumpled-up aluminum can at me. It bounced off the filthy rags I'd draped over my chest.

Couldn't do it. Wouldn't do it.

They'd kill me, though, if I didn't. If they found out.

It had seemed like a good idea, at the time.

No, that's a lie. It had seemed a stupid, gross, inhuman idea from the get-go. But the *only* idea. The only way to get out of this hell, let alone the only way to save Val.

I turned my head. The mud and gunk with which I'd coated my face cracked and flaked off in places, but that was okay. Made me look authentic. Like I was losing skin in the dry, desert heat. My disguise fooled the livies, and somehow it fooled the deadies, too.

That was the part I'd been most worried about. Rick said that they could sense us, that they homed in on the signals our brains gave off or something. I didn't know if these ones were decomposed beyond that, or if the Fat Man just had them so well-trained that the only time they'd chow on a livie was when it was a competition or a prize.

Either way, my ruse had gotten me in. Fooling the livies had turned out to be the easy part. Whenever a livie died, rather than burn the corpse, the guards moved it over to the corral before it could reanimate. They weren't exactly diligent about checking for vital signs, either. I'd made like I had been hiding a wound all along, played dead, and *voila*. In among the deadies.

Maneuvering to be one of the contestants had been a little trickier, but it had worked. Here I was, competing for a tempting prize.

I could see Val in the flabby circle of the Fat Man's arm. He was feeling her up, squashing her against his blubbery side.

Val looked on the verge of tears and that decided me. I had to do it, no matter how sick it was. For her. Then she'd finally look at me and *see* me, see and appreciate the real Scott Driscoll.

The deadie beside me was gnawing on the side of a hollowed-out head, trying to peel off a flap of scalp. One of the handlers was there to inspect the empty hole of the cranium.

"Done!" the handler shouted, thrusting his fist in the air.

More people hustled forward. With movements born of practice and efficiency, they unlatched the empty, popped in the refill, and scrambled out of the way as the deadie dove in for seconds.

The stock of a gun rammed into my back. I barely stifled a cry. Had to remember not to react. *They* didn't feel pain.

"What's the matter with you?" the gun-wielder snarled. "Eat up."

"Done down here!" came another cry.

The crowd was clapping rhythmically. On my right, the female deadie was trying to get the last tasty morsels from the bottom. She popped up, triumphant, with the medulla oblongata hanging out of her mouth, and jerked her head in quick succession like a bird, gulping it down.

I was losing. I wasn't even on the board yet.

Liver. I'd eaten liver before. Once, on a hunting trip, even deer liver, raw and dripping from the carcass.

If I'd done that, I could do this. For Val.

The handler jabbed me in the back again and this time I bent forward, toward the rippled folds of brain tissue.

My dad had given me the crappy old family station wagon for graduation. When the deadies started ambling, we stashed guns and other supplies in the wagon. Canned food, camping gear, blankets.

Everybody laughed at us, you bet they did. Even Val had, at first. But she'd stopped in a hurry when her mom came home from the beauty shop one day and tried to open her head with freshly-manicured acrylic nails.

No one was laughing now. There weren't enough people *left* to laugh.

The station wagon had held up like a trooper during our entire crazy escape and flight south. Now, as I pulled over to the side of the road, its engine let out a sort of weary rattle. The tires sent up a huge plume of dust and soot.

The girl came running up to the car. "Thank you, oh, thank you, I thought you were going to drive by and leave me, thank God you stopped," she said.

She was giving me big adoring my-hero eyes. I thought for a minute she was going to hug me, maybe even give me a big my-hero kiss to go with it. If she'd been a babe, enough to make Val jealous, I would have been all for it.

The others had climbed out of the car and were looking around nervously. Jess had the shotgun and pushed his glasses up, squinting. Sharon clung to the dog's bandanna. The girl introduced herself as Patty.

"You'll be safe with us," Rick told Patty, puffing up his chest.

It was kind of funny to see him trying to act all manly. I mean, he's been my friend since grade school, but I'd never had any delusions about either of us. Smart, okay. Jocks, we were not.

"Let's not stand around all day," Jess called. "I don't see anything moving, but ..."

"But yeah. Back in the car," I said.

The smell was acrid and meaty and awful. I hadn't been aware of it before, not with the stale stink rising off the deadies and the rancid sweat of the crowd.

I could even smell the fine-ground bone dust and the charred, cauterized skin left by the bone saw. The inner membrane – I hadn't even known there was such a thing, but I'd seen them snip through it with kitchen shears – was peeled to the sides in neat folds.

Streaks of blood were drying on the surface of the exposed brain. It had been wet, glistening, when they first clamped the livie into place before me.

The desert sun was baking it. If I waited too long it would get tough to chew.

My eyes closed. My mouth opened.

I thought of liver. Of oysters. And, of course, of gelatin. Always room for it, wasn't that how the ads went?

A curved, quaking surface touched my lips. I skinned them back from my teeth, which had never needed fillings or braces. That had to give me an edge on the average deadie, whose teeth were chipped or broken out from chewing on bone.

For Val.

I took a big, slippery bite.

I steered in and out of traffic jams, cars and trucks that had been abandoned, overturned, smashed into scrap. Heaps of rotting food strewed the sides of the highway, spilled from produce trucks. The only movement besides ours was that of countless scavenger birds and animals, feasting with impunity.

That, and the windfarms. Talk about creepy. Miles and miles of posts with spinning pinwheel blades, whirring around and around. Generating electricity for a dead world.

The station wagon labored as it chugged up to the pass. I wasn't the only one to heave a sigh of relief when we made it over, and started downhill.

High desert country. Home of military bases and Shuttle landings, Joshua trees and borax mines. In the twilight, the desert valley was a brownish-purple smear cut by the ruler-straight line of Highway 14.

We descended toward Mojave, hoping there might be something worth finding in that strip of gas stations and burger joints. Thinking about food, lulled by the hazy scenery, I didn't see the pileup until Patty squealed a warning.

I stood on the brakes. The only reason none of us were thrown into the dashboard was because we were packed in so tight.

Two semis had jackknifed, and another few cars had rammed into them, entirely blocking the road. The station wagon shuddered to a halt less than a foot from the bumper of a VW van.

"Everybody okay?" I asked, my voice embarrassingly unsteady.

Various replies of assent reached me. I saw a turnoff to the left, and a BB-pocked sign reading 'Joshua Flats, 6 miles,' with an arrow.

"Can we get around?" Jess asked from the back.

"Shoulder's too soft," I said. "We'd get stuck."

"Well, think of something, brainiac," Val said.

It squelched between my teeth. The texture was hideous, like soft-boiled eggs with striations of chewy gristle. The taste was bad, too, but the texture ...

The man clamped into the wooden frame went stiff, then began to jitter and twitch. A fresh stink of voided bladder and bowels wafted up. I could hear his jaw clenching until bone cracked.

I took another bite. Determination drove me onward. Once the initial deed was done, the first step taken, the revolting sin committed, it got easier. Don't ask me why or how. All I knew was that I'd gone this far, and continuing wasn't going to make things worse. Instead, quitting would. If I quit and it was all for nothing, that would be really losing.

The noise of the crowd was louder than ever but I ignored it. I ignored the sporadic cries of "Done!" from the handlers. I was in this to the end, and I was going to win it.

Blood pooled in the bottom of the man's skull. I thrust my face in to reach the rest of his brain and wolfed it down. Something in my own brain, some switch or fuse, had blown with a snap and a sizzle.

"Done!" someone near me cried.

I straightened up, chin smeared with blood and cerebrospinal fluid and other assorted goo. They switched victims with the professional speed of an Indy 500 pit crew and a fresh one was locked into place. I dove in, tearing out ragged, dripping chunks.

Thoughts shut off. I was an animal, a machine. I bit and swallowed, bit and swallowed, barely bothering to chew. My throat worked. My stomach hitched once, in shock maybe, and settled down.

I had the advantage, and not just for my teeth. I had tendons that weren't withered and stretched. I had functional salivary glands. I had a whole tongue, an esophagus that wasn't riddled with decay.

Most of all, I had the motivation. I wasn't doing this out of hunger or habit. I was in this to win.

We were able to push the VW van out of the way, but it didn't make quite enough room for the station wagon to get by.

Jess turned to me with a questioning look, maybe about to ask which one we should try next, and that was when the deadie reached out through the broken windshield of one of the semis and clawed the side of his face clear down to the bone.

He stood stock-still for a second, his questioning look turning into a gape. His blood was pouring onto his shoulder, raining onto the blacktop.

The deadie's sticklike arms shot out again, seized Jess, and yanked. He flew backwards through the glass-ringed gap and into the truck's cab. He dropped the shotgun. Sharon shrieked.

Deadies swarmed over the wrecked vehicles and the girls were screaming and the dog was barking. Jess's despairing howls echoed from inside the truck.

I had time to notice how weird they were, the deadies, how different from the ones we'd seen up north. Those ones had been green, moldy. If you hit them in the middle, they'd belch out clouds of dead gas. These deadies were dry, their flesh shrunken, their skin leathery. They looked like mummies. Scarecrows. Beef jerky. The arid heat did that, I realized, and then they were on us.

"The guns!" I yelled at Val. "The other guns are in the back!"

Rick panicked and went tearing off into the desert with two deadies in pursuit. The movies always showed them all shambling and slow, but these ones were fast. Rick was moving faster than I'd ever seen him move in my life, running like he'd made the track team. Didn't matter. They caught up with him, bore him down, started eating him alive.

A deadie woman with brittle peroxide hair leapt on Sharon. Another lunged at me and I danced back, tripped, and almost went down. If I had, that would have been the end. I kept my footing, cracked my crazybone on the side-view mirror of the station wagon, and kicked out. My foot struck the deadie in the hip and spun it around.

"The guns!" I yelled again.

Val looked at me, all big blue eyes and wide, surprised mouth. She dove into the car.

She slammed the doors, and locked them.

I couldn't believe it.

"Here!" Patty cried. She shoved a stick into my hands.

A deadie in a California Highway Patrolman's uniform came at me, still wearing his mirrored cop-shades. His mouth opened and closed in vicious snaps. I swung that stick like I was in the World Series, and missed by a mile. The effort spun me around.

I pulled Patty with me, our backs to the car. I hammered on the window.

"Open up! Open up, Val!"

The CHP snagged Patty's sleeve. She batted at his hand and yodeled a high-pitched cry. I brought the stick down across the deadie's forearm. Both stick and arm broke in half.

"Val, goddammit!"

Deadies were fighting over the bodies of Sharon and the dog. Others were converging on Patty and me. One snared a handful of Patty's hair. She flailed as if a bat was caught in it. Dry fingers splintered off, caught in her hair like grotesque barrettes. Another deadie darted at her with gaping jaws.

A little-kid deadie bit my leg. I yelled and punched down, the broken-off end of the stick still in my grasp. It punched through the top of the kid's head. Frantic, I probed at my leg and found the heavy denim of my jeans undamaged.

Through the dirty window, I could see Val. She wasn't doing anything useful, like maybe getting the other guns and saving our asses.

The deadies pulled Patty away from me. She was reaching out, begging for me to save her. But others were rocking the car, trying to flip it, trying to get at Val. I shook off Patty's trailing, grasping hands and wielded my broken stick like a truncheon.

A riflecrack split the air. A deadie pitched over, skull bursting apart to reveal a brain like a deflated football. The others froze, shoulders tucking up defensively. Patty, gasping and sobbing, scrambled to my side.

More guns went off, a chattering fusillade of them. Puffs of grit kicked up from the ground. Deadies went down in ruins of desiccated flesh.

I stared incredulously as a bastardized vehicle roared into view like some sort of escapee from *The Road Warrior*. It was painted a mottled brown, desert camo, and guys – livies – in camo jackets and helmets stood in the turret, blasting away at the deadies.

When they had dealt with the deadies, they leveled their guns on Patty and me.

An astonished hush fell as I ate, ate, ate. Gorged.

The handlers struck at the deadies with batons, urged them to keep up. The one on my right succeeded in swallowing down another half a brain and then paused, mummified face taking on a queer look. A moment later, the leathery skin of its belly parted and its overstuffed stomach flopped out through the slit, tore free, hit the planks of the platform, and popped.

Masticated grey matter and deadie digestive acid sprayed the front row of the crowd. A split-second later, the same thing happened to the deadie at the end of the line.

I ate. Blood and brain-pulp covered me to the hairline, to the ears. My own stomach felt hugely bloated, smooth, and strained. Busted a gut, funny how you heard that term all the time but never quite like this.

"Done!" my handler shouted. "What's the score?"

"That's five," the Fat Man proclaimed from on high, where he had Val crushed against his sweaty folds. "A new record!"

"Sev-en, sev-en!" the crowd chanted. That was my number, the one that they'd hung around my neck when I shuffled onto the platform with the others.

"How much time left?" my handler asked.

"Still two minutes."

"What do you say, dead boy? Got room for more?"

He didn't wait for an answer. A fresh victim was secured, the exposed brain not so neatly prepped this time. They'd run out of pre-made meals. They were grabbing people out of the crowd, doping them, and sawing off the tops of their heads just to keep up with the demand.

Before I could make sense of it, the guys in the armor-plated SUV had grabbed me and stuffed me in back. Two soldiers stood watch on Patty and me while the rest broke the windows and dragged Val out of the station wagon.

We tried to talk to them. Livie to livie and all, how we were all on the same side and should stick together and all that good stuff. Nothing helped.

They took us to the town, which had been ringed with walls and barbed wire and booby traps. At first I thought it was to keep the deadies out. But the defenses were there to keep *us* in.

The deadies were kept in some sort of old barn. They gravitated to the fence of their corral, not touching it after they'd gotten a couple of zaps from the electrified wires, and stared vacantly through.

The town was full of livies, most of them prisoners. Some were from town, others had been nabbed off the highway. The men and women were kept separate. I hadn't seen Val or Patty since we arrived.

I got the lowdown from a local. Big Joe Callup, also known as the Fat Man, had been Joshua Flats' chief of police until his compulsive overeating, and subsequent weight gain, had forced him onto disability. Fat? He was beyond obese, circus-freak fat. He couldn't even get around on his own, but rode instead in the back of his customized pick-up. Sort of a post-apocalyptic sedan chair.

When the world ended, he took the town hostage. He set up his own little kingdom, with hand-picked soldiers and weapons from the National Guard armory. Raiding parties brought in supplies, more prisoners, and enough deadies to keep them entertained.

"Entertained how?" I asked, not really wanting to hear.

"All sorts of ways," my new acquaintance said. "He has them fight each other. He maims them and races them. Sets them on fire. Bull-riding. Rodeos. Football games. He's the emperor, they're his gladiators, and this is his private Coliseum."

"What about us? How do we figure in?"

"Us?" He smiled bitterly. "We're the prizes."

The final buzzer sounded its harsh bray a millisecond after I gagged down the final hunk of my seventh brain. Seven for lucky number seven.

"The winnah!" Big Joe exclaimed.

The livies were cheering like they meant it. Anybody who didn't make a sufficient show of enthusiasm was liable to be put on the auction block for the next event.

I wasn't concerned about the next event. All that mattered to me was getting through it, getting Val, and getting out of here.

The guards had spread the news that she would be the next prize. The juicy ones were usually chosen early because a shapely or muscular bod inspired the slavering deadies to a better effort.

I'd already witnessed one of the events of 'entertainment,' and I'd seen what had happened to the prize, a steroid-type fitness junkie. He'd been torn to pieces by the winning deadie soccer team.

That couldn't happen to Val. I couldn't let it.

I knew I'd only have one chance to save her. And escape, before it was my turn to have a ribbon around my waist.

The deadie competitors struggled as the bar came back up, but listlessly. They were full, and trained enough to know what came next. Those that were still mobile would go back to their stable. The ones who'd exploded their overstuffed guts would be taken to the edge of town, and burned.

I tried to act just like them. I let my shoulders slump, my head loll, my stare go vacant. Inside, though, my pulse was skyrocketing.

I'd won. The prize – Val – was mine.

She was enough to make any deadie feel lively again, all that rosy, lush, firm flesh jiggling about.

The handlers led me toward the Fat Man's pick-up truck. Just like they'd led the deadie soccer team up to claim their reward.

I tried not to let my excitement show. This was it. This was my chance.

Big Joe lolled in the truck bed like a sultan, on a bed of old sofa cushions and futons. The rig had all the comforts of home. A tarp on metal poles kept out the worst of the sun. A cord snaked through the cab's rear window, plugging the mini-fridge into the cigarette lighter. The area around him was littered with crumpled pop cans, candy wrappers, and half-empty bags of salty snacks.

He was a human behemoth in sweat pants that could have housed a family of four, and a ship's sail of a tee shirt with a beer company logo on it. Nearly lost amid the bulges and jowls was a hard, mean face that might have once been handsome.

His arm was still around Val, his greasy hand squeezing whatever he could reach. The up-close sight of him touching her almost made me lose it.

"You won a pretty piece of prime cut, here, boy," he boomed down. It was more for the benefit of the crowd than for me, I hadn't a doubt. His eyes were bright and merry, demented Santa Claus eyes.

I snatched a glance at the pick-up's cab. The engine was idling to keep the battery from running down, lest the Fat Man have to suffer the misery of warm soda. The windows were down.

Deadie. Had to act like I was a deadie. I gazed at Val with an expression of slack-jawed greed, while trying to make meaningful eye contact with her.

She wouldn't look at me.

Deadie. Deadie. I shuffled closer to the truck and let a guttural noise come out of my throat. I belched.

That was a mistake. The heavy churning weight in my stomach sent up a vile bubble and I was tasting the brain meat all over again. My throat hitched. I suddenly knew I was going to spew a geyser.

Somehow, I held it down.

First, Val.

The Fat Man howled with laughter. "Looks like some boy's still hungry. Want your prize, sonny?"

All around me, I could hear livies crowding close, cheering, egging me on, even placing bets as to what I'd bite first.

Out of the corner of my eye, I saw a familiar, pallid face, framed in limp blond hair.

Patty. The moment I looked at her, I saw her recognize me. Her eyes got wide, her mouth dropped open, and I knew she was about to blow the whole deal.

I caught her eye. If ever a guy had wished for telepathy, it was me, and it was right then. I silently urged her to stay cool, begged her not to blow my cover.

Her chin quivered. I saw her throat work as she fought down a gag. But then she gave a slight nod. She understood.

Good girl. Smart girl.

Time to move. It was my only chance, the chance I'd been waiting for.

I'd have to be quick in order to take them by surprise. First the handlers, while they were distracted by Val. Shoulder them aside. Slam shut the tailgate with Val still in there.

And then run around to the driver's door, jump in, and take off. With Val safe in the truck, and the Fat Man as a hostage to get us past the guards and out of town. Next stop, anyplace but here.

I could do it, I knew I could. They weren't expecting any surprises from a deadie. The walking meat in the pens were too well-trained. They knew better than to move against the handlers, or other livies, unless the situation called for it. I could thank that little bit of conditioned response for keeping me alive.

"Here you go, honey-bunch," Big Joe chortled. He nudged Val toward the tailgate.

She stumbled on chained ankles, fell to her knees. A hurt grunt escaped her. She looked up through a veil of hair and saw me. Really *saw* me. Just like with Patty, her mouth dropped open and my name was poised on her lips.

I shook my head, trying to make it look like a deadie nerve-jittering impulse. My hungry-sounding moan was a warning.

"Uh-uh-uh," Val said, chains clanking as she trembled. She knew me. "Suh ... skuh ..."

No! No, oh, goddammit!

Sudden spiking fear made my stomach's heavy cargo slide and bubble. Because that was *hope* dawning on Val's face. Hope, and joy, and all the things I'd always wanted to see in her expression. Just not now!

A wavering lunatic's laugh issued from Val. She started to smile, started to reach out toward me.

She was ruining everything! People were looking at me more closely, seeing the solidity of my flesh – scrawny, maybe, but not dried deadie flesh.

"Shut up," I said, low but urgent, under a rising murmur from the crowd. "Shut up, Val."

Any second, suspicion would turn to certainty and that would be all she wrote. And all because Val couldn't get with the program.

A line of phantom pain lanced around my skull. It traced a curve where the bone saw would grind and scream. Poetic justice, they'd think. I would feel the ripping of capillaries as they took the top of my head off like a layer of sod.

The stupid bitch! We were so close! So close to getting out of this with our lives, and she couldn't play along for two minutes?

A glottal howl burst from me. After everything I'd done, after the horrible thing I'd done, and this was the thanks I got!

"Scotty –" Val said, but her weak voice was drowned out by my furious cry. No one else could have heard.

But I did.

She called me Scotty. Again.

I lunged for her, shouldering the handlers aside just like in my plan. Even better than my plan, because in my surge of angry strength, I sent them flying. I seized a handful of Val's thick dark hair and dragged her headfirst out of the pick-up.

The Coliseum, my acquaintance had said. Like in the days of ancient Rome. I remembered something else they did in Rome. After a feast.

I turned my head to the side and stuck a finger down my throat. My body heaved. A torrent of hot cerebral slush surged up my gullet and splattered everywhere.

I had to make room.

The handlers took me to the barn. I could barely walk, my gut feeling bloated. I had consumed a lot of fresh meat. Would probably be days picking the strings of her hair out of my teeth.

I hadn't been able to get through her skull. My jaw just couldn't apply that sort of bone-cracking pressure. I'd had to go for the neck, instead.

And then, once she hadn't been able to talk any more and blow my cover, I guess I sort of went a little nuts.

They put me in with the deadies again. I was too stuffed and lethargic to worry about whether my disguise and their training would hold up. One or the other must have, because none of them made a move against me.

Or maybe, on some instinctual level, it was because they recognized me as one of their own. I had never actually *died*, but inside, I was a deadie all the same. I had to be. No genuine livie could have done what I had.

A few days later, when I was finally starting to feel physically back to normal – mentally and emotionally, I was as much a deadie as ever – they brought a new one to the barn.

Thin. Limp hair that might have started out blond. She had sunken cheeks and hollow eyes, and her skin was mottled with stains under the rags of her clothes.

Not a bad disguise at all.

But then, I knew Patty was a smart girl.

She stood near me, neither of us speaking, as we stared with the deadies out through the fence at the town, and waited for the next event.

THE BARROW-MAID

THE DEATH-CRY OF SVEINTHOR Otkelsson ripped through battle-clangor, as harsh and sudden as the blade that had ripped through his mail-coat.

Friend and foe, ally and enemy, all who heard it fell silent. The fighting ceased as men looked to one another, astonished.

Could such a cry truly have come from the throat of Sveinthor Otkelsson? Sveinthor Wolf-Helmet? Sveinthor, called the Unkillable?

He had led the first assault against the shield-wall in defense of his uncle Kjartan's fortress, plunging deep into the armies of King Hallgeir the Proud. Arrows had rained all around him but never once touched his flesh. He had beheaded Hallgeir's standard-bearer, then cleaved Hallgeir himself in the shoulder so that the king's torso was hewn nearly to the belt.

A death-cry? Sveinthor Otkelsson, voicing a death-cry?

It could not be believed.

No one moved. No living thing made a sound. Even the cawing of ravens was stilled, and it seemed that the wind itself paused in scudding dark clouds across the sky.

Then, as one, those nearest Sveinthor drew back. He stood alone amidst a mound of bodies, most slain by the thirsty work of his own sword, Wolf's Tooth. And the blood ran thick from his belly, spreading over the earth in a wide red stain.

He was Sveinthor Otkelsson, whose ship *Wulfdrakkar* had gone a'viking to far lands, bringing back plunder of gold and silver, slaves, amber, ivory, and jet. He had rescued the beautiful Hildirid from becoming an unwilling bride, unmanning her captor with a knife-stroke.

Even if not for the *wyrd* that had been prophesized by the sorceress Sigritha when Sveinthor was no more than a boy, this moment could not have been foreseen.

But now Wolf's Tooth had dropped from his grasp, and his hands went to his wound, and the blood was a waterfall between his fingers. His wolf-headed helm, its gilded nasal and eye-pieces red-spattered but still glittering gold, turned this way and that, as if seeking out his killer.

A single raven screeched. All who heard it knew it to be an omen of the most fearsome sort. The raven was Odin's own bird, and surely Odin had taken notice of the battle. Perhaps Odin was, even now, dispatching the dreaded Valkyries.

Then, as Sveinthor toppled, with his belly split open and the tangle of his guts spilling out of him, there came another cry, furious with rage. It was torn from the throat of Ulfgrim the Squint, long a friend and blood-brother and oathsman of Sveinthor.

In his fury, Ulfgrim charged. Rallied by his actions, the others of Sveinthor's men followed, as did Kjartan's own forces. What came next was not so much battle, as butchery. Some of the defenders tried to form again their shield-wall, but too many fled in terror, and the rest were soon cut down. The victors moved among the fallen, giving aid to their allies and the final mercy to their enemies, and stripping the dead of their valuables.

Kjartan, himself, aged and white-bearded, rode from his fort to the place where Sveinthor had stood. He wept openly and without shame. There had been talk in the mead-halls that Kjartan might make Sveinthor his heir. Now that hope was gone, dashed to pieces like a ship storm-hurled against unforgiving stony shores. Sveinthor was dead. With his last breath, he had closed his blood-soaked fingers around the hilt of Wolf's Tooth, and held it now, in an unbreakable grip.

They bore him back to Kjartan's hall. The day was won, the enemy scattered and fleeing, but there was precious little joy and celebration.

Three others of Sveinthor's men had perished bravely in the battle. Eyjolf Rust-Beard, Bork Gunnarsson, and Thrain the Merry were to be placed alongside Sveinthor, in honor.

Kjartan had for them a great burial-mound built, a chamber filled with goods for the afterlife. There were bundles of firewood, jugs of mead, furs and blankets, tools, weapons, grain, meat and cheese. Into this tomb was placed Sveinthor's wealth, the plunder of villages and forts and monasteries. Silver cups and platters, gold brooches, piles of hack-silver, beads of amber and jet. Kjartan added many more treasures, so that the mound was as rich as any gold-vault of the Dwarves below the earth.

Sveinthor was laid upon his barrow, at the center of the chamber. His helm was polished and shining, the wolf's tail that hung from its crown brushed smooth. He was covered with the pelts of wolves, and his sword, Wolf's Tooth, was set across his breast, its hilt still clutched tight in his dead hand and its blade still clotted dark with the blood of his enemies.

As these preparations were being done, Ulfgrim the Squint sought out Hildirid, who had been Sveinthor's woman.

"Kjartan has promised to provide a slave-girl to accompany Sveinthor into the mound," he told her. "There is no need for you to die with him."

Hildirid, who was tall and slender but proud-figured, said nothing. She had hair the color of gold seen by torchlight, which fell past her waist in long plaits tucked through the belt of her tunic. Her cloak was seal's skin, pinned at the breast with a brooch of walrus-ivory, and her eyes were sea-blue and steady.

"You can escape this dire fate," Ulfgrim urged her. "Already, Kjartan's wise-woman is preparing the poison. You have but to agree, and the slave-girl will go in your place."

"Does not Unn of the dimpled cheeks go with Eyjolf, her husband?" Hildirid asked. "Is not Ainslinn, Bork's favorite, being readied to follow him? You would have Sveinthor, who loved you like a brother, go to his grave-barrow with a stranger slave-girl?"

"Thrain does," argued Ulfgrim, "for Thrain had no woman of his own, and will need one to tend him in the afterlife. You can live, sweet Hildirid. Live and go forth from here, and marry a strong man and have many fine sons and fair daughters."

He touched her hand then, but Hildirid drew away. "I was fated to be his and his alone, forever," she said. "Skarri the Blind prophesized it to us. It is my *wyrd*."

Ulfgrim scoffed. "And we have seen for ourselves how well the *wyrd* prophesized for Sveinthor came to pass. Mad old women and blind old men, pah!" And he spat on the ground.

"I was fated to be his," Hildirid said again.

"There is no fate but what a man makes his own. Sveinthor went wrapped in the confidence of his *wyrd*, and it did make him bold and daunted his enemies, but in the end, did his *wyrd* prove true? Look there, Hildirid. Sveinthor the Unkillable ... covered with gold and glory, but as cold and dead as a haunch of beef." He clutched at her hand again. "Come away with me, instead. I may not be so handsome as Sveinthor, but I swear I can love you as much, if not better."

This time she did not merely draw away, but slapped him so that her palm cracked smartly across his cheek. "I will follow Sveinthor," she said, and her voice was like ice.

Ulfgrim flushed dark, angered and embarrassed. His eyes, already narrow, narrowed further. "It was I who learned of your capture," he said in a snarl. "It was my cunning that formed the plan to rescue you. I would have done it myself, but Sveinthor insisted. By rights, Hildirid, you should have been mine."

She walked away from him then without a word, head high and back straight in her dignity.

Later, when the burial mound was all but finished, Kjartan assembled his people to bid farewell to Sveinthor and his men. There were many verses and poems spoken by skalds, recounting the deeds and honor of their lives, mourning their passing and celebrating their entrance into Valhalla.

Then Kjartan's wise-woman brought forth the cups of poison. Unn of the dimpled cheeks drank first, and kissed Eyjolf's lips before lying down beside him. The woman Kjartan had chosen to accompany Thrain smiled at the great honor she had been given as she raised the cup. Thrain's favorite dog, a great shaggy mongrel called Bryn-Loki, was strangled with a rope and set at his master's feet.

The slave-girl Ainslinn wailed and screamed and would not drink. She tried to flee, then tried to fight, and finally had to be strangled as Bryn-Loki had been. A disgrace, but only to be expected from an Irish girl and a Christian.

And then the cup came to Hildirid, who was arrayed like a queen, with her long hair loose and shining.

As she took the cup, she saw Ulfgrim with his dark eyes pleading. But she drank deep of the bitter liquid, and as she felt its lassitude begin to creep through her limbs, she kissed Sveinthor and sank down next to his barrow, on a blanket of soft wool.

She opened her eyes to the chill, misty dark, and felt a pain all throughout her body so sharp and crushing that it was as if she was being rent asunder by beasts. It was Niflheim, kingdom of the dead, realm of the goddess Hel. And was it Hel's own hound, Garm, grinding her bones in its fierce mouth? Was it the dragon Nidhug, leaving off its eternal gnawing at the roots of Yggdrasil the World-Tree?

Then the pain ebbed like a tide, receding from her limbs. Hildirid shivered in the blackness. Her mouth felt dry and parched with a terrible thirst, and her innards were a hollow ache.

Slowly, stiffly, she moved. The cold wrapped her like a fog, and she pulled her cloak close around her shoulders.

The air was heavy with a reek of corruption, so thick it was like a taste. Yet, beneath it, she could smell other scents. Strong cheese. Heady mead.

Her dark-blinded hands sought out carefully over the unseen contours and edges. Soft wool. Hard stone. Rushes and pebbles and loose earth. Stacked logs of wood, the bark coarse beneath her fingers. The lushness of fur. Wolf's fur, from the pelts that covered Sveinthor, and that was when she knew where she was.

In the barrow. In the burial-mound. Entombed in the black, entombed with the dead.

And was she dead? Was this death? Was this the truth of Niflheim? Alone and sightless and trembling from the chill?

Yet she breathed, and when she pressed her hand to her breast she could feel the quick thudding of her heart. With the little knife she kept on her belt, she pricked her thumb and felt warm blood well from it, which she licked away.

Still carefully, groping her way, she rose to her knees and found Sveinthor's chest beneath the pelts. She touched the silver Thor's-hammer amulet he wore around his neck, touched his wiry beard, touched his face.

His flesh was like a lump of cold tallow, greasy with a residue that smeared off onto her fingertips. His mouth gaped and did not stir with breath.

Hildirid rested her brow on his chest. Then she searched blindly through the goods in the barrow until she had a candle, and the means to strike a flame.

The flickering light sent shadows dancing over the wealth and the weapons and the bodies. Unn and the slave-girl were peaceful in death. Ainslinn had died with her eyes bulging in horror, the bruises from the knotted strangling-rope livid on her slim neck. Bryn-Loki, Thrain's dog, lay with tongue protruding and death-rigid legs jutting like sticks.

The smells of corruption wafted from them. Hildirid saw skin gone waxen and pallid, flesh sunken and slack. They were dead, dead one and all ... and yet she was alive. Somehow, she was alive.

She had drunk of the poison. She had drained the cup to its very dregs. It had coursed through her veins. She remembered sinking, sinking like a rock, into the bottomless depths.

Her gaze fell upon the jugs of mead, the loaves, the wheels of cheese. Hunger led her to pull off a chunk of bread, but Hildirid hesitated with it at her lips.

Should she? Was there any use in eating, in drinking? Why prolong a life that was doomed to a miserable end?

Better if she ignored the urges of her body and lay back down to wait for death. Better still if she took out her knife again and seated it in her breast or sliced it across her wrists, to hurry death along.

Yet the bread was in her hand. It was stale and nearly as hard as stone, but could not have been more appetizing had it just come fresh from the baker's oven. She tore into it with her teeth, and when it soon proved a chore to chew, opened a jug of mead and soaked the bread to soften it in the potent honey-brew.

Sated, she moved the candle so that its light played over the various treasures. Here was a tiny ship, the *Wulfdrakkar* in miniature, with red shields along the sides above the tiny oars, and its growling wolf's head prow. There was a set of *hnefatafl*-men, two armies carved from ivory and soapstone, arranged in ranks on their board. A bone flute. A polished-amber figure of a wolf. Chests of silver and gold. Monk's crosses.

A heavy silver plate with designs of Christian saints and angels upon it.

A fortune, and all of it useless to her now. Likewise were the many weapons useless. What need did she, Hildirid, have for bows and arrows, axes, shields, and spears? What need for swords? She had her knife, the knife of ivory, hilt wrapped in gold wire, and it would do as well as any blade for what she might have to do.

How the men had given good-natured jest to Sveinthor when he'd given it to her! "Provide your woman a weapon," they had said, "and you're all but inviting her to use it on you, should you displease her as all men eventually do."

But Sveinthor had never displeased her. They had never quarreled, not once. He had never raised a hand against her. When he had sought counsel, he had listened to hers with as ready an ear as he had that of any of his men. He had been as fervent in love as he'd been in battle.

And when his death-cry had rung out, it had been her own ending in that instant.

Yet here she was, alive among the dead. Sveinthor would be in Valhalla, and she would not be there to serve him. Who would bring him the great drinking-horns and joints of roasted meat dripping with good juices? Who would arm and armor him when the final call came and Odin's forces assembled against the giants?

She retreated to his side and sat there, huddled in her sealskin cloak. The candle burned low and went out. When hunger and thirst again bestirred her, she rose to take a few bites, a few drinks of mead. Sometimes she would bring out her knife again, and set its point to the swell of her breast, but each time – to her shame – her courage would slip from her.

Now and then she lit another candle, but the sight of the treasures did not gladden her spirits, and the sight of the dead as their flesh continued to darken and decay only brought her to despair.

Even in the darkness, though, the dead would make sounds. Tendons creaked as rigor stiffened and relaxed their limbs. Gases gurgled within their bloated bellies. Once, a rancid and rattling corpse-belch produced such a stench that, inured though she was to the odors of the mound, Hildirid was made to vomit up her meager meal.

At last she became aware of new noises. She heard a scratching, like that of rats ... faint at first, but gradually growing louder. Next came a harsh grating and scraping, as of metal on stony soil.

And Hildirid understood.

Word of the wealth of Sveinthor's death-hoard must have spread far and wide, the value increasing all the more in the telling, until at last it had won the interest and greed of the lowest kind of dishonorable men. Grave-robbers, armed with shovels, come to plunder from the dead. To steal away the gold and silver, the amber and ivory, the cups and platters and other treasures. They would strip the corpses bare of their mail-coats and arm-rings. They would have Wolf's Tooth from Sveinthor's cold grasp, if they had to break off the brittle, rotting husks of his fingers to do so.

In silence and utter darkness, for she by now knew her way as well as she'd ever known her own house, Hildirid took up her knife and went to wait by the entrance. She could hear the digging-sounds louder now, and the voices of the men. As they dug, and cleared away more of the earth, their words came readily to her ears.

Hildirid was left aghast at all that she heard.

Kjartan's enemies had returned in greater numbers than before, aided by treachery as some of the king's own men turned against him. The mighty fort had fallen. Hundreds of men had been slain, their weapons and valuables taken, and their bodies left unburied.

Now Kjartan's feasting-hall rang and thundered with the revelry of his foes. They gorged on food from his store-houses and drank his mead by the barrel. They butchered his goats and pigs, forced the surviving men to fight like bears or horses for their amusement, and made slaves of the women and children.

Worst of all, Kjartan himself had been seized prisoner. Night after night, he was made by his captors to appear in one humiliating costume after another. Fool's garb, a monk's robe, the clothes of a woman ... these things, they dressed him in, and led him before the men, who laughed and called and hurled refuse at the white-bearded king.

Such mistreatment of the man who had been kindly as a father to Sveinthor filled Hildirid with anger and hate.

Then she heard clearly a voice that she knew.

"If she is dead, old woman, I'll hang you by your heels from a tree-branch and leave your body to be picked by the ravens."

The voice belonged to Ulfgrim the Squint, and it was answered by the cracked and peevish tones of Kjartan's wise-woman, who had prepared the poisons.

"I did as you wished, noble lord," she said. "I mixed in her cup a potion of deep-sleeping, but I told you that you would have to be quick in fetching her out of the tomb before its effects wore off and she woke. I told you that! If she has starved, or died of the cold, it is no fault of mine!"

"Peace, brother," another voice said, and Hildirid knew this one as well. It was Halfgrim the Thief, bastard half-brother to Ulfgrim. "If she is dead, she is dead. There are other women, and fairer, we can find for you. Wealthy as you are now, you can have your choice of them, and never mind that you are ugly as the rump-end of a troll."

Rough snorts and laughter greeted this, though not enough to keep her from hearing Ulfgrim's next words. "I will have Hildirid," he said. "Or I will have none other."

The deadly determination in his voice made the laughter stop for all but Halfgrim, who chuckled all the more. "Then I hope for your sake the maid lives, or she'll be a bedmate even stiffer and colder than the ones you're used to. Myself, it's Sveinthor's gold that I want."

"And I," said another voice, one that Hildirid did not know, "want only to piss on his rotting bones for what he did to my father."

"As a favor to me, then, Runolf," Halfgrim said, "be patient and save your pissing until I've gotten off his mail-coat. It should fetch a pretty price in silver, for all it has that hole ripped across the guts."

Runolf, she knew, must be Runolf the Younger, whose father's skull Sveinthor had crushed with his shield-boss in the battle. So Ulfgrim had joined with the traitors, and Ulfgrim had seen to it that the poison in her cup had not been poison at all.

"Yes, yes," Ulfgrim said, aggrieved. "And the blame for that hole, we all know, you lay on my head."

"I do, indeed, brother," Halfgrim said. "You were supposed to slash his hamstrings and then skewer him through the neck. What made you stab him in the belly?"

The very breath in Hildirid's lungs had turned to frost, and the blood in her veins to water as icy as that of the far northern seas.

"I had no choice," came Ulfgrim's reply. "He realized my intent at the moment before I would have struck, and had I not sunk my blade into his guts, he would have had off my head."

There was more talk as the digging continued, but Hildirid paid it barely any mind. At last the shovels met wood, and were laid aside, and she then heard the splintering crash of axes against the planks. They broke inward. Torchlight poured through the gaps, bright as the brightest sun's rays to her, long accustomed as she was to blackness and feeble candle's flame.

The first man to step through was not Ulfgrim, but his half-brother, his gaze fixed greedily on the glitter of gold and the sparkle of silver. Halfgrim never once looked her way, until her knife-blade plunged down. He wore no mail, and she embedded the steel to the very hilt in his chest.

Halfgrim screamed like a woman in childbearing and staggered back, then fell, sprawled at Ulfgrim's feet. The knife had been yanked from her grip and now Hildirid faced them weaponless, but the sight of her revealed by the torches held the men shocked and motionless with terror. A hag she must have been, a filthy crone, with dirt on her clothes and her hair hanging in strings and clumps, her eyes as wild as those of a raving berserker.

Then some fled, casting aside their torches and tools into the crude trench of earth they had made to reach the barrow-mound.

"You see?" said the wise-woman. "She lives, as I told you."

Ulfgrim stared at Hildirid, and spoke her name in a strengthless voice. He stepped over Halfgrim and offered out his hand.

"Traitor," she said to him. "Foul, murdering traitor! You killed Sveinthor!"

"I did it for love of you," Ulfgrim said.

She flung herself at him, though not in the lover's greeting for which he had hoped. Her nails, long and ragged, raked at his face and dug long furrows in his stubble-bearded cheeks. Ulfgrim grappled with her, his strength far more than a match for hers, and soon held her with her arms bent painfully behind her back.

Runolf the Younger pushed his way past them as Hildirid struggled in Ulfgrim's grasp. "You men! There is the treasure, the reward you were promised. I will have satisfaction for my father's death."

"What of Halfgrim?" another asked.

"Leave him," Runolf said. "It is a burial-mound, after all." He turned with torch raised high, so that its light was shed over the central barrow.

And there he stopped, for the corpse of Sveinthor was sitting upright.

The wolf's pelts had fallen away to the earthen floor. His torn mail gaped where the fatal blow had been struck, and through it could be seen the bulging maggot-ridden fester of his entrails.

His eyes, no longer clear blue but clouded and murky as if rimed with muddy ice, peered around from within the gilded eye-pieces of his helm.

Then Sveinthor rose to his feet.

Some of his guts slipped from him, swinging against his thighs like a grisly apron. His joints groaned and his bones crackled. Bits of his skin had sloughed away, leaving raw muscle glistening. His lips had peeled back from his teeth, giving him a leering death's rictus of a grin.

The sword, Wolf's Tooth, he still held in his hand, and he extended it now in challenge and invitation.

"*Draugr!*" the wise-woman cried, and threw herself to her knees, babbling prayers to Thor and Freya and Christ and to other gods of which Hildirid had never heard tell.

It was a word most used when a man was lost at sea and denied decent burial, so that his restless corpse was doomed to wander. Sveinthor had not drowned, but he was *draugr,* nonetheless.

A fierce joy sang within Hildirid's breast, and she cried her lover's name. "Sveinthor!"

"Kill him!" shouted Ulfgrim, retreating and pulling Hildirid as he went.

Runolf had dropped his torch and snatched out his own sword. As the other men rushed forth, waving their axes and shovels, shrieking their horror at this unnatural foe, Runolf hacked down at Sveinthor's shieldless left arm and severed it at the wrist.

No blood gushed from the stump. There was a trickle of thick blackish ooze, and a fresh whiff of stink. The hand fell to the ground and twitched there, then turned itself over and began finger-clawing toward the oncoming men.

Wolf's Tooth flashed down, and Runolf the Younger spun away with his face sliced open. From cheekbone to chin, it hung down in a flap of bleeding meat, exposing his teeth and gums.

But the others were urged on by desperation and terror, and raced wildly at Sveinthor. One of them trod upon the severed left hand, which skittered up his leg, swift as a spider. His charge became a frantic leaping dance as he beat at himself with his shovel, hoping to dislodge the scrambling hand. He was too slow. It vanished beneath the hem of his tunic and crawled to his groin, where it squeezed and mauled and twisted like someone wringing water from a rag. The man squealed.

A hoarse and rumbling howl came from Sveinthor's throat. Though distorted, it was still familiar. It was his battle-cry, his call to arms.

At the sound of it, one by one, around the burial chamber, his loyal men rose in answer. Eyjolf, with an arrow still jutting from his eye socket. Bork, the knob of his shoulder-bone showing through pulped and mangled flesh, where his arm had been cut off. Thrain the Merry sprang up, almost eagerly. They seized the weapons with which they had been laid to rest, and took their places at Sveinthor's side.

Their women rose, as well. Faithful Unn of the dimpled cheeks ... not dimpled now, but sagging, and the foam of the poison dried to a crust on her lips. The slave-girl, a little creature and young, but hissing like a cat. Even Ainslinn, head lolling on her puffed and swollen neck, got slowly to her feet.

And the battle was joined in a furious clangor of metal and screams. The close confines of the burial-chamber became a slaughtering-ground. Flesh struck wetly on the floor, and blood flew like sea-spray in all directions. The *draugr* women had no swords, not even knives, but they had teeth and fingernails and fists, and a strength that seemed more than the equal of any two mortal men.

Ulfgrim had seen enough, and fled, dragging Hildirid with him. In her last glimpse of the scene within the mound, it looked almost to her as though the risen dead were not merely fighting their foes, but devouring them ... tearing off mouthfuls of meat, lapping hungrily at the blood-spatter, even nuzzling their faces into the guts of the fallen to come up with steaming livers and intestines clenched in their jaws.

The night outside was foggy and damp, turning the distant torches on the walls of Kjartan's mighty fortress to golden smears of elf-light. Though she fought him with every step, Hildirid could not win her way free of Ulfgrim's iron grasp. He pulled her into the broad field, the both of them stumbling over broken spear-shafts and split shields and the scavenger-picked remains of the unburied dead.

"Let me go!" demanded Hildirid, trying to bend back his fingers where they held hard around her wrist.

"They're monsters, you foolish sow!" Ulfgrim shouted. "Did you not see? They'll kill you, or eat you alive!"

"I'd rather that death, than life with you!"

But he would not release her, even when she fell, full-length, and tangled in a pile of corpses. Taking her by a fistful of hair, he made as if to sling her over his shoulder and carry her the rest of the way.

Then a long shaggy form hurtled out of the swirling fog and slammed into him, ripping his hand loose from Hildirid's hair and leaving long strands caught in it. He was knocked, hard, to the wet earth, where a shadow-shape loomed over him.

It was Bryn-Loki, Thrain's dog, who had never liked Ulfgrim. Parts of his fur had fallen out in patches, and the rest was slimed green with mold. He smelled dank, and horrible. The growl that came from low in his throat was bubbled and strange. His teeth, though, when he skinned his black lips back from his muzzle, looked strong, and sharper than ever.

Ulfgrim rolled into a crouch, drawing his sword. It was, Hildirid suddenly knew, the same one that had struck Sveinthor that treacherous, fatal wound. Now he thrust it into Bryn-Loki's chest as the dog leapt. The blade sheared through ribs and muscle and gristle, loosing a spurt of foul fluid. Bryn-Loki fell, shuddering, onto his side. Ulfgrim got up, shaking but sneering victoriously, and wiped the reeking blade on the dog's thick fur.

Bryn-Loki raised his head, snarled, and clambered to his feet. He shook, the way a dog will after a hard rain, and more fur dropped in mangy clots from his hide. Stiff-legged, he advanced on Ulfgrim, who turned again and ran for his very life, as if all the fiends of Niflheim were close upon his heels.

There were no fiends except Bryn-Loki, but Bryn-Loki was fiend enough. Hildirid, kneeling amid the dead, watched the chase as Ulfgrim made for the safety of the earthen wall around the fort. The churning mist had nearly hidden them when she saw Ulfgrim madly scaling the wall, and Bryn-Loki make a final lunging leap. His jaws snapped, tearing a chunk from Ulfgrim's buttock. Then Ulfgrim was up and over, gone from her sight.

The dog trotted back to her. As Bryn-Loki came, the first stirrings of fear gathered in her belly. She wondered if it would hurt, the rending of his teeth. She wondered if it would be quick.

She closed her eyes as his paws thumped to a halt on the damp earth, only a few paces distant. It seemed she could smell Ulfgrim's blood on his snout. A cold nose bumped her, snuffling thickly. Then a colder tongue, wet and reeking with decay, lapped at her face.

Hildirid opened her eyes. Bryn-Loki sat hunkered on his haunches before her. His head was cocked, his tail making jerky, lurching wags, as if he could not quite remember how to do it properly. When he saw her looking at him, he uttered a hollow whine, and the wagging became so energetic she worried his tail might fall off.

Other figures appeared through the gloom. They were drenched in blood, and gobbets of flesh clung to their garments and hair. She knew them, and as they neared her, she stood to face them, with the dog sitting beside her and her hand resting on top of his head.

Eyjolf's leg had been hacked to the bone, so that he staggered along nearly lame, leaning on Unn, who swung a tattered scalp of long grey hair – the wise-woman's hair – from her hand.

Bork, already lacking one arm, now carried his own head tucked into the crook of the other, his eyes blazing fiercely. Ainslinn could no longer walk, but pulled herself over the earth by her arms. The little slave-girl who had been buried with Thrain held a man's forearm, and munched happily at it as she might have gnawed a pork rib. Thrain himself wore looping strings of intestine around his neck, and his grin was wider than ever.

And with them came Sveinthor. His mail was shredded and his body scored with countless cuts that seeped and oozed. He still held Wolf's Tooth, a dark red rain falling from the blade. His severed hand rode upon his shoulder, like one of Odin's ravens.

Hildirid went to him, and embraced him, but then stepped back, for she knew that his work was not yet finished. He surveyed the battle-field, strewn as it was with the unburied dead, and once more raised his hoarse voice so that it rang and rolled like thunder.

In the fortress on the hill, there was much commotion and alarm. Perhaps when Ulfgrim had come in, they had dismissed his claims as drunken ravings or madness. But now as, one by one, the corpses of Kjartan's slaughtered army laboriously rose and armed themselves with what makeshift weapons they could find, the living men flocked to the walls with many torches and stared out in horror.

Sveinthor strode among them. They formed into ranks and lines below the earthen wall and the approach to the fort. At the front was a shield-wall, the shields splintered and broken as they overlapped. With slow but inexorable, relentless purpose, the walking dead began their advance.

A storm of arrows descended upon them, and though many found their mark and lodged in flesh, they could not do much harm. Some of Sveinthor's *draugr* were so bristling with arrow-shafts by the time they reached the base of the wall that they looked like hedge-hogs, and still they advanced.

Hildirid stood atop the burial mound, her hair and sealskin cloak streaming around her in the dire wind that had sprung up. Bryn-Loki sat at her side, and her hand still stroked his head and scratched his ears, for he was whining in disappointment at having been left behind from the battle to guard her.

Now, from the fort came flaming arrows, but many of the *draugr* had lain so long in the rain and mud that they did little more than smolder. One or two, fatter men in life, burned like tallow, and became shuffling candles in the shapes of men. The smoke from their singed hair and charred, rotting bodies blew back over the wall, filling the fort with an abominable stench.

At last, a few of the bravest defenders came out to meet their foes, but they soon fell, and the *draugr* swarmed over the wall and into the fortress. Even from where she stood, Hildirid could hear the cries of pain and anguish and terror, and the ghastly sounds of feeding as Sveinthor's followers feasted on quivering, still-warm flesh.

Later, when quiet had descended and the night was almost done, she took Bryn-Loki and ventured into the fort. Everywhere she looked were *draugr*, plundering the newly-dead and adorning themselves with medallions and arm-rings, or taking trophies of scalps and fingers and jawbones and heads. The living – the women and children and slaves taken from among Kjartan's people – cowered, unharmed and ignored.

Then she saw Kjartan himself, freed from his prison and seated upon his great wooden chair, draped with bearskins. Ulfgrim's body, bound in ropes, lay before him with a pool of blood around the stump of his neck. His head was held aloft on the point of Wolf's Tooth, raised high by Sveinthor.

Kjartan saw her, as well. "He will not stay, Hildirid," the king said. "He must return to the burial-mound, before dawn comes. He has fulfilled his *wyrd*."

No amount of imploring by them could sway Sveinthor. As the sky to the east brightened, the *draugr* left off what they were doing. Almost as one, they left the fort and returned to the field, lying down again where they had died and then arisen. Eyjolf,

Bork, Thrain, and their women entered the tomb, followed by Bryn-Loki.

Only Sveinthor remained. He had Ulfgrim's head knotted by the hair to his belt, and Wolf's Tooth was finally released from his grip to be sheathed again across his back. With his one good hand, he reached out and caressed the curve of Hildirid's cheek. Then he turned from her, and walked toward the mound.

"Farewell, lord," Hildirid said to Kjartan, and kissed him.

"Hildirid!" the king called. "Where do you go? What do you do?"

"As you said, lord, Sveinthor has fulfilled his *wyrd*." She touched the knife at her belt, and smiled. "Now I shall fulfill mine."

So saying, she followed Sveinthor into the darkness. When the sun rose, the entrance to the mound was covered over again with planks and stones and earth. Never again was it disturbed by mortal men.

And so ends the saga of Sveinthor the Unkillable, and the beautiful Hildirid, his beloved barrow-maid.

CURED MEAT

THE DEN IS COOL, the dirt sandy and dry beneath us. We stir. Slow and sluggish at first, bodies stiff, joints cracking, tendons creaking.

Day. Sunshine as we emerge. Early warmth baking into us, easing away the night chill, the lethargy.

Those with good eyes and ears take turns at sentry duty. Watching. Listening. Alert for anything that might mean danger ... or prey.

We are all very hungry.

We are always very hungry.

But first, we must groom.

There are ragged edges, peeling flaps, dangling pieces. There are stringy ends of veins poking out, tough gristle, splinters of bone. There are crunchy little worms that tunnel deep, crawling ants, clumps of maggots to be scraped from damp crevices, bug-kind that lay eggs in us.

The damp is bad.

The damp makes us soft, spongy, loose. The damp makes us slimy and green. The damp makes us rot.

We groom.

Fingers and teeth. Pinching, plucking, nipping, gnawing, nibbling. Skin scraps, bits of flesh, parasites. We rub with sand to scour and dry. We dust-roll. We turn to follow the sun.

The small or weak or damaged do their part. They attend the big and the strong and the whole. Even those who become too impaired to be useful are good for one final thing.

We are all, always, very hungry.

The meat of our own kind fills, but never satisfies. We are sun-dried, salt-crusted, smoked. Hard to chew.

The meat of bird-kind, bug-kind, beast-kind, fish-kind ... that meat fills and *almost* satisfies. Almost.

Once, there was other-kind. Like us, but not like us. Moist and warm. Supple and sweet. With dark-hot-rich pumping blood. With juicy organs cradled in layers of succulent fat.

Their meat ... their meat filled *and* satisfied.

But they are long gone.

Their great den-places are burned and flooded, rusted and crumbled, barren and overgrown. Bad places. Dangerous places. Full of sharp things that snag and cut, heavy things that fall-crush-break, hidden things that roar and explode in fiery thunder. Holes, pools, pits. Bad, dangerous places.

Sometimes, our kind still go there. Drawn by habit, by hunger, by hope. Searching for the other-kind, for the meat that fills and satisfies.

A few who go, return. Most who go, do not. None who go, find.

There are only rumors.

Always, rumors.

Rumors of strongholds where other-kind gather behind high barricades, with weapons that can skull-shatter from far distances. In the strongholds are dens that stay bright and hot and dry as a summer day, even on the wettest winter night. In the strongholds are plump and tender other-kind, protected by fast and powerful other-kind.

Rumors of a single enormous many-denned structure, where water leaps and fabulous things glitter, and all is splendid decoration, and there the other-kind are packed so numerous that we could eat and eat and eat until our guts burst. An endless feast.

Rumors.

So many rumors.

None true.

But some of our kind believe, and even go. Hoping. Hungry.

Always, always so very hungry.

We groom as the sun climbs. The burly one, sitting on a sand pile above the den's opening, has a freshly-split scalp. It hangs in a tattered fold over a shriveled ear. Dull bone shows through. Damaged ones cluster around the burly one. Our leader. They are servile and deferential, eager to please, currying favor.

The legless one tears away that patch of skin and tangled hair. Offers it back to the burly one, who ignores it. The tiny shrunken one darts in to snatch at the morsel, misses, scrambles up the legless one's torso to grab again. They squabble until the burly one cuffs them both. Absently. With a grunt of annoyance. The half-faced one takes advantage of this show of displeasure to sidle in and resume the grooming.

There was a recent battle. Another group. Territory and dispute. We stood tall, with arms upraised to seem larger, we groaned and wailed to seem fearsome, and when they would not give way, we fought.

We won.

We drove them off. We brought down two of them, crushed their heads, ate their meat. A salt-crust and a smoked. Some of us were scratched, gouged, bitten. The burly one's scalp was split. Some had fingers broken, dry-snap like twigs. But we won.

Our group is strong.

Our leader is strong.

The legless one chews and chews, jawbone working, straggles of skin and hair hanging out of a mouth-corner. The tiny shrunken one crouches nearby, poised to lunge for any tidbit that falls. The half-faced one finds a swelling on the burly one's shoulder and squeezes it between hard thumbnails until a pebble-sized tick is forced out, and the half-faced one eats it.

A sentry gives an alarm and all grooming stops. We wait, ready.

Dirt and brittle brush. Ridges of coarse stone. Dunes and cracked-parched gullies. The wide-above sky, no clouds, no damp, no sense of coming damp. Faraway shapes of bird-kind. The intense fireball of sun.

No challenge-call from a rival group. No help-call from one of our own. No entreaty-call from a stranger wanting to join us, or the hail-call of a wandering one come with news and rumors.

The air is silent, hot and still. There is only the whir and hum and click of bug-kind. It makes us hungry. Even for that poor meat.

We wait.

Some of us – hopeful, foolish – cannot keep from searching for a sign of the other-kind. The sound-throb-vibration of their machines, their music, their weapons, their voices.

Hopeful. Foolish.

There is a group, we know from more rumors, who fed on other-kind that came from the sky in huge shining things. That group has stayed ever since, basking on sun-heated strips of black stone, waving the sticks that once summoned the huge shining things down from the sky.

Very hopeful. Very foolish.

Very hungry.

Always, so very, very hungry.

The sentry gives the alarm again. A threat-warning. Long dry growth rustles and ripples. Dust puffs and drifts. The low forms of beast-kind appear. Narrow, lean, and rangy. Matted pelts. Muzzles and teeth. Flat yellow eyes.

They growl their hate of us. They hunker and piss wet-yellow in their fear.

The burly one heaves up from the sand. The biggest one and the tall quick one also shake off or push away their attendants, and rise to face the beast-kind.

So do I.

The marked one.

The marks cover my arms from wrists to shoulders. They go all around my torso. Dark whorls and intricate lines. Smoke-black and blood-red. Like shadows beneath my skin. Symbols. Images.

Some believe that the marks protect me, keep me safe. The marks are why I have lasted so long, and stayed so whole.

There is a small-finger missing on one hand, the stump charred over. A chunk is gone from my calf, the wound an irregular scoop where the flesh was bitten away in a greedy mouthful. An ear-rim was torn off in some battle.

The beast-kind piss and growl even more as we confront them. They want to leap upon us and rip us to pieces. They want to flee from us as fast as their four legs will carry them. They would not eat our meat but shun it, kick dirt over it, squirt more of their yellow fear-piss onto the ground where it is buried. If they did bite off and swallow some part of us, they would vomit it out and *then* kick dirt and squirt piss.

All of the beast-kind fear and hate us.

They know we are hungry. They know we want to kill them and gorge ourselves on their meat that fills but does not quite satisfy. They know we would seek out their vulnerable little ones, eat them helpless, blind and squeaking. That is why they fear us.

They know we are not the other-kind. That is why they hate us. That is why they would destroy us, if they could. If they found one of us alone or unwatchful, they would attack. Tearing with jaws and claws. Goring with horns. Kicking and trampling with hard hooves.

All of the beast-kind ... but these ones ... these beast-kind who once shared dens with the other-kind, who remember them as we do, who search for them as we do ... they hate us most of all.

We are not alone, and we are not unwatchful.

We are many, and strong, and ready.

The burly one raises both arms, and groans at the beast-kind. Daring them. Inviting them to come and try, come and try, we will peel their hides and break their bones and pull out their guts, we will scoop their eyeballs from their sockets and pop them sweet and juicy in our teeth.

The biggest one does the same. So does the tall and quick one. So do I.

So do the sentries, and the attendants, and the rest of our group. Soon we are all standing tall – those of us who *can* stand – atop the dunes and hills around our den. Standing tall with arms raised, groaning and wailing.

We are too many for them, too strong, too ready. But they are too many for us, too fast, too agile. A fight would be costly for both sides, and we all know it.

The beast-kind shrink and slink and finally retreat into the long grass. The burly one's arms come down. The sentries go back to their places. The grooming continues.

I sit with my leg bent, inspecting my calf. The hole is not deep, but it is tricky, and sometimes damp collects there, or the bug-kind burrow into it no matter how often I scour it out with sand. I present my back to the hollow one, who picks carefully, so as not to damage the marks that cover it in their intricate smoke-black and blood-red designs.

Only the hollow one has the patience and precision for this. Only I find the hollow one useful enough to keep.

The hollow one is sun-dried and frail, scant meat clinging to thin bones. Knuckles and elbows and knees and chin are exposed where stretched-taut skin has split or worn away. Below the ribs is a gaping open cavity. No organs nestle there except for a single dusty and deflated lung. The spine is a knobby ridge. Strands of gristle and cords of muscle crisscross like thick webs, helping to hold the hollow one's upper and lower halves together.

At last the day's heat shines full upon us. The shadows are chased away. The grooming is finished. We can forage and hunt.

Some stay behind to guard our den, and the ones who cannot move well. They will dig and clean. They keep watch. The rest of us follow the burly one, our leader.

Bug-kind, we eat as we find them. Into the mouth, crunch, a spurt of bitterness and the barest teasing taste of meat. Ants and grubs. Long wriggling many-legged things. Spiders and scorpions. Hard-shelled beetles. All too squirmy to carry back to the den alive, and too small to bother carrying back dead.

There are bird-kind that can be eaten in a single bite, and bird-kind with wings as wide as our outstretched arms that can be shared. There are eggs hidden in nests beneath bushes, or up in the branching forks of trees ... eggs that are so delicate a wrong grip can crush them into a warm-runny-gooey mess flecked with bits of shell. Not exactly *meat*, but good just the same.

Fish-kind, we do not often find, because fish-kind will only be where it is wet, and we stay far from the wet places. Creeks that flow and trickle, or pools that are deep and still ... those are bad.

Then there are beast-kind. From the small and quick to the large and lumbering. Lone stealthy hunters and huge massing herds. Long coiled ones, with scales and darting tongues. Slow-moving ones, with soft meat inside bony plates. Furry bodies with skinny naked tails. Spiny-bristly-pokey ones.

We hunt. We forage. Alert for the pack that had come near our den to growl their hate. Crunching bug-kind and small birds, not finding much else. Two of the bony-plated ones, a few long-coiled ones. A single large bird ... but not large enough.

The first large beast-kinds we see are of a kind we have often tried to hunt before, and usually failed. Like the pack of beast-kind that came to growl at us from the grass, these ones hate us as well as fear us. If we go close, they will rear up and kick out and knock down and trample flat.

We range farther. Following the burly one through a territory that seems almost empty, knowing what this means. Knowing we will have to leave our den and move on. Into the changed and the unfamiliar. New territory, new den, new rivals, new threats.

But ... new meat.

For meat, we would do whatever we had to do.

So very hungry.

The sun is at its highest when the burly one leads us to a place where the ground is cut by a narrow straight flatness. An other-kind thing from the days long gone.

It is hard like stone, dark like stone. Where it is not covered in dune-drifts and sheets of sand, it holds the sun's warmth well into the night. But we rarely come here, because it is the edge of our territory.

The battle was here. The burly one grinds teeth and rubs at the spot where the scalp was torn into that hanging ragged flap.

The bones are mostly as we left them, scattered on the hard sun-warmed flatness. Some have been buried in wind-blown sand, some taken away by scavengers. But most are still there. Stripped of every speck of meat, the long legbones cracked and sucked clean of marrow. We left skulls smashed like eggshells, the dense meaty brains scooped out and triumphantly de-voured.

There is another other-kind place on the far side. The remains of a structure, with bright-sharp glints in the corners of square holes. Stout posts. Round rings made of some solid black stuff, even harder to chew than the tough flesh of our own kind. Jumbles of rusted machine-parts. Long snarls of thorny wire.

We pause, alert for trouble. The wind blows gritty, swirling sand and sending bristles of dry bush bouncing past.

A fur-covered, long-eared beast-kind hops and sniffs, hops and sniffs. A few small bird-kind dart and flit. Nothing else moves.

Our rivals seem nowhere nearby.

The burly one beckons, commands. We follow. Onto the flatness and heat. The air ripples around us. Puddles of not-wet glimmer in the distance. The sun is hot and good.

We cross the flatness. Beyond our territory, now, into theirs.

The tall quick one makes a sudden lunge at the long-eared beast-kind. It goes rigid in terror. Then its nose twitches, its hindlegs spring. But that instant of terror was enough. The tall quick one has it. A single wrenching bite and the beast-kind's throat is gone. Its hindlegs kick-flail-jerk, go limp.

Meat.

Not much meat. Not enough meat. And we are all so very hungry.

Two mouthfuls each. Fresh warm meat and slippery guts. Tufts of fur pasted to our faces by sticky crusts of drying blood.

We move on.

Toward the crumbling structure made by the other-kind.

The biggest one objects.

The burly one commands again, with rising irritation.

We all know that sometimes there is food to be found in such places. Strange food-relics left by the other-kind, encased in metal that is bulged and weakened and distorted, easy to break open. Sometimes the food within is even meat of sorts … the meat of fish-kind or bird-kind or beast-kind … never the meat of other-kind … and most of the time it is plant stuff, inedible … but sometimes there *is* food.

This is the burly one's argument.

But sometimes there are dangers in such places, even ones as small as this. The other-kind may have left their strange encased foods, but they also left points, hooks, and cutting edges. Things that could damage us. And if there *was* food, surely our rivals had found and eaten it by now.

This is the biggest one's argument.

The rest of us gather and wait.

The burly one is our leader, has been our leader for a long time. Ever since the large hairy one chased a beast-kind along a steep slope and was swept down in a rockslide, limbs broken, skull smashed, brain spread in sticky lumps over a boulder.

The biggest one would like to be leader. To have the most attendants for grooming, the driest spot in the den, the choicest bits of meat. To give the orders and make the decisions.

The burly one has been a brave and strong leader. We have held our territories, won many battles, increased our numbers by overpowering weaker rivals and bringing their best into our group, while feasting on the remainders.

But we have taken risks and suffered losses. There have been hastily-dug dens that seeped with rain, bringing damp-rot. There have been battles and hunts gone wrong. The foraging has become poor, the meat scarce.

We wait as they argue. The metal-toothed one and the skinny one take up sentry posts because this is rival territory, but the others stay with the tall quick one and me.

The biggest one had been a leader once, not of our group but of another.

Leader of a group we fought and beat. With ease.

Not all of them with such ease. Not the biggest one. The biggest one damaged several of us in that battle. The biggest one had wrenched the short stocky one's head off with one hard twist and hurled it, caving in the tall slow one's chest in a splintering burst of ribs.

But then we had beaten the rest, and the biggest one surrendered and joined us.

They go back and forth, the burly one and the biggest one, until the noseless one interrupts with an alarm.

An urgent, hungry alarm.

Beast-kind. A herd of them on the move, stirring up a haze of dust. Hunched backs and swishing tails. Horns curving out from their low heads, some blunt and stubby, some long and sharp. Large and solid.

Meat.

So much meat!

The argument is forgotten.

We go.

The beast-kind plod slowly, eating the dry brown grass. As we get closer we can feel the thud of their hooves vibrating through the ground. Bug-kind buzz around their eyes and ears.

They are huge and heavy. A single one could fill us all.

Fill, but not satisfy.

They are nervous. They shift and snort.

Some of us want to attack. Others want to be cautious.

The burly one attacks.

Arms raised. Groaning and wailing.

We follow.

The beast-kind are startled, afraid. Their hooves pound the earth, flinging up clods of dirt, billows of dust, shredded grass. They bellow. It is a milling churning mass of meat, horns, and hides ... and we are in the middle of it. Grabbing, grasping, reaching, clawing.

Then there is blood. Thick dark splatters of blood.

A horn-tip catches my hip, tears my skin, knocks me spinning. My feet tangle. I fall to the shuddering ground with beast-kind thundering all around me. A hoof slams down beside my head. Just misses.

I grab for the leg attached to that hoof. The beast-kind stumbles, trips, drops with a shaking thud. I yank myself up and on. There's a broad dusty expanse of hide in front of my face. Short coarse hairs atop skin. The heat of a live-thing, the beast-kind's side rising and falling, a frantic beating throb from inside, where its organs are.

My jaws gape and I bite. That coarse hair, that tough hide, resisting my teeth and then giving way. Now there is more blood. Thick and dark, in a gush this time, into my mouth, pouring down my chin.

The beast-kind heaves and lunges but I hold on. I bite deeper. Meat against my teeth now, meat in my mouth, meat sliding down my throat as I gulp it in hot ragged chunks. Others are with me, leaping upon the beast-kind, tearing at it while it squalls and kicks.

We eat. Ripping and pulling. Blood everywhere, blood all over us, damp and wet, but there is *meat*, meat and a loose flood of guts when its belly comes open, and we eat and eat and eat.

Finally we are full. Not satisfied, never satisfied, but full.

The herd has gone. Two beast-kind are dead in flattened grass and blood-muddied dirt. We are full and there is still so much meat, more than we can carry, more than enough for the ones back at the den.

But the burly one is not with us.

Bug-kind buzz around us now. Landing to sample the blood. We are damp with it and now there are bug-kind and we badly need grooming.

But the burly one is not with us.

Not eating with us.

Not giving orders for carrying meat back to the den.

Not reminding us that we must groom.

Not leading us.

Not with us at all.

And the biggest one is damaged. Gored. Horn-gouged. A deep hole punched into a shoulder, and another to the groin. One arm hangs useless, the bones snapped in many places.

The noseless one makes a call, not an alarm but a help-call.

We go.

The burly one's body is far from the kill-spots, as if dragged there. Dragged there, impaled, then dropped or dislodged or shaken off. The horn-gouge must have gone in through an eye socket and out through the top of the head. Bone-slivers jut up from the scalp.

The skinny one crouches and pokes probing fingertips into the wound, then, when there is no reaction, grasps the edges and pries the skull apart. It cracks and splits. The skinny one scoops out the punctured brain, digging under until the stem is severed, and holds it out in cupped hands.

There is a long moment of uncertainty.

Our leader is gone.

The biggest one is damaged.

It is the tall quick one or me, now.

The long moment stretches longer.

Uncertainty. Indecision.

With sudden resolve, the skinny one peels the brain into segments and passes them around to everyone. We may be full, but we still eat. This settles things for now. Anything else must wait until later.

Then the metal-toothed one gives another alarm.

This is not our territory. Our rivals are coming.

We cannot fight them, so we take as much as we can carry. The best meat, dripping slabs of it. Rich organs – liver, kidneys, eyes, tongue. We load ourselves until we are bent double and staggering from the weight. The rest of the meat, we have to leave for them. The burly one, except for the brain, we also leave.

Already, bird-kind circle overhead and swarms of bug-kind have appeared. Soon, more beast-kind like the pack from before will arrive to scavenge their share, if our rivals do not get there first.

They come but we go. Hurrying. Burdened with meat. The biggest one may be too damaged to ever fight or hunt again, but one arm still functions enough to carry much meat. Out of the grasslands. Back to the other-kind place. Across the long narrow flatness. Into our own territory. Returning to our own den.

Eating. Grooming. Standing sentry.

The wobble-headed one stays near the biggest one, but the burly one's former favorite attendants are uneasy, their positions within the group now precarious. The legless one pulls arm over arm along the ground, staying meek and submissive, toward the tall quick one. The half-faced one attempts to lick the congealing blood from my torso, but the hollow one is there with a hard shove and a warning snap of the teeth, and the half-faced one cowers. The tiny shrunken one snatches up a whole liver that the noseless one dropped and scurries off with it, down through the den's entrance and into some side passage too small for the noseless one to pursue.

Neither the tall quick one nor I take the spot atop the sand pile, above the den. Not yet. It happened too fast, too unexpectedly. No leader. It will be one of us, must be one of us, but we do not know which, and dare not make a presumptive move too soon.

We eat. We groom. The sentries keep watch. We dust-roll to dry and cake the blood, then pick it away. I inspect the horn-scratch on my hip. The smoked flesh is ripped and uneven. The bone is nicked. But it is not bad damage. I can still walk. I can still hunt and fight.

The hollow one needs only a single chunk of meat. It goes in the mouth, is chewed, is swallowed, goes down the throat, and drops into the gaping cavity where the pieces can be fished out and eaten again. Over and over. Until that single chunk of meat has been reduced to a mashed-up pulp. The hollow one is never full, can never be full, but the act of eating is enough.

The sun descends toward clouds. The air begins to cool and there is a hint of dampness to it. We feel night's approach in the growing heaviness of our limbs, the stiffness-sluggishness-lethargy that creeps into our bodies.

We enter the den before the last of the sun's warmth has ebbed from us, and settle into our accustomed places in the sandy soil.

The next day brings rain. We stay below, where it is dry. We are cold and hungry, but we stay.

The day after that brings sunshine again, sunshine raising steam from the wet earth. Also raising many bug-kind from the wet earth, and we feed on them eagerly.

A decision has been made. The tall quick one defers to me. So do the rest of the group. The biggest one does so grudgingly, but does. I am the new leader. I sit atop the sand pile. The hollow one grooms me and will not allow anyone else to help.

A sentry gives an alarm. Then there is a hail-call. It is a wandering one, seeking permission to come near. The rest of the group waits for me to grant or deny that permission.

I grant it.

The wandering ones belong to no groups, because no groups will have them, and they form no groups of their own because even the wandering ones do not like to be together. They go alone, from territory to territory, visiting for as long as they are welcome, sharing what meat will be shared with them, and then they move on, bringing news and rumors from one group to the next as they go.

The damp cannot damage the wandering ones, cannot make them rot, because they do not rot. They are not smoked or salt-crusted or sun-dried like the rest of us, but they still do not rot. They are ... preserved somehow ... some way we do not understand.

Beast-kind shy away from them and bug-kind do not infest them. They can be damaged as easily as we are, sometimes *more* easily. They can be destroyed by a crushed skull or mangled brain, just as we can. But they are not the same as us.

The sour reek of chemicals lingers around them in a miasma. Liquid oozes from their skin, beading like dew. Their eyes are milky and sunken behind loose, drooping lids. Some have long straight cuts from collarbones to breastbone and down the torso, the edges held together by metal clamps or loops of thin dark cord. More strings, these often pale and hair-fine, dangle from the soft, torn flesh of their lips.

Their meat is vile and inedible.

This one is pallid and ashen and bloated and slick. Like the belly of a fish-kind that has bobbed to the surface of some deep wet pool. There are no straight cuts on the body, but one eyelid is gummed shut and the lips are shredded.

I grant the wandering one permission to come near and join us for a while. If there is news, even if there are only rumors, I want to know. I need to know, if I am to be leader.

Most of the beast-kind meat was already consumed, but there is chewed pulp left in the bottom of the cavity where the hollow one's guts used to be. As a token of hospitality, I scoop some out in my fingers and offer it. The rest of the group offer worms and beetles. The wandering one eats, slurping and smacking with those shredded lips.

News. News that seems like rumor. But the wandering one insists that it is true.

A group, not far from here, found the other-kind.

We do not believe. Not all of us. Not immediately.

True, insists the wandering one. Not rumor. True.

Some of us *want* to believe.

The wandering one claims to have been there, claims to have seen-smelled-heard. Not to have tasted, not to have eaten, because while we might share ordinary meat, no group would share something as rare and precious as other-kind meat.

Warm, breathing, bleeding, tender, juicy, succulent other-kind.

Meat the way meat should be. Meat that fills *and* satisfies.

If it was true ...

If only it was true!

The wandering one insists that it is. Suggests that we go there, find out for ourselves. The wandering one will show us, will help us fight the rival group if we must, and in exchange, wants a few bites. Just a few bites.

It is tempting. Very tempting.

Our territory is hunted-out. We must move on anyway. We must move in some direction. There will be disputes wherever we go. The chance at other-kind meat ...

The noseless one groans. Imploring. Hungry.

The rest of the group join in.

I decide. We will go.

So we go.

Those who can move well help or carry those who cannot. The hollow one stays by me, and the wandering one walks with us. I have the metal-toothed one, whose eyes are very good, keep watch.

That night we shelter in a ravine, beneath a rock-shelf over-hang. The next night we must huddle together in the open, unhappy and exposed under a dark sky of fierce bright spots. There has been little meat, no time to hunt. But the beast-kind who might attack us smell the sourness of the wandering one, and avoid us, instead.

At last we are close. We are in their territory. The plants are short and squat and spiny. The stones rise in pillars and arch-es and strange shapes. There are stinging bug-kind and swift long-tailed bird-kind that run along the ground. We find a cave that is large and dry, roomy enough for us all.

I send the metal-toothed one ahead with the wandering one, with orders to return and bring me news. Real news, not rumor.

They do not return that day.

They do not return the next day.

We are all restless and uneasy. There are squabbles over the scant meat of bug-kind and running bird-kind. The biggest one is belligerent, mocks my inaction. The tall quick one does not agree ... but also does not disagree. The tiny shrunken one bites the legless one, gnaws off most of a hand, leaves the legless one too damaged to be useful. There are squabbles over that meat, as well.

I must do something.

I summon the tall quick one and the skinny one. We will go. The rest will wait.

We leave the cave when the sun is high. Bird-kind circle in the distance and we move toward them, until we find the place.

The carnage-place.

Parts everywhere. Rot everywhere. The ground stained with dried fluids. A rippling, humming cloud of bug-kind roils above it all.

The wandering one is there. We cannot tell if the metal-toothed one is there. Many more are there, though. All of them in pieces. Decaying under the hot sun, decaying in that roiling bug-kind cloud. Salt-crusted meat, smoked meat, sun-dried meat ... maybe even other-kind meat ... it doesn't matter. All of it rotting. All of it seething with maggots, teeming with flies.

Then the tall quick one gives an alarm.

Movement.

Tottering, staggering movement.

Approaching us.

The mouth flaps. The lips and tongue gabble. There are sounds and wild gestures, pleading, begging.

It does not have wrappings over its skin, wrappings that might be fine and flimsy or sturdy and tough. It is not plump and pink, jiggling with rolls of fat. It is as naked as us, thin and dirty, scabbed and scarred.

But it is other-kind.

Other-kind!

We go.

We go with arms raised and outstretched. We go groaning and wailing.

And hungry.

It pleads and begs, then stops, and turns, and runs.

The tall quick one brings it down. It screams. It thrashes and kicks. Then the skinny one and I are there. We grab. An arm in my hand. Warm. Pulsing with life. The other-kind screams and screams and *shrieks*. Fingernails dig and gouge. Blood flows. The tall quick one tears off a dripping chunk of thigh. The skinny one claws at the belly.

I bite into the arm.

Meat!

Meat like nothing else!

Moist and delicious!

Gobbets of it bulging in my cheeks, sliding down my throat. A thick vein throbs between my teeth, throbs at a furious beat, then bursts as I clamp down. A gush of rich blood spurts from the corners of my mouth, streams over my chin and chest.

We eat. We feast. We gorge.

The screams and thrashing finally stop.

We keep eating.

I remember the rest of the group at the cave, waiting for us, but we keep eating.

The meat is very salty. But it fills. It *satisfies*.

I pull open the other-kind's slack mouth to reach in for the sweet spongy tongue, and I pause.

The tall quick one is slamming a legbone against a rock, to get at the marrow. The skinny one is rooting around in the guts. They do not notice.

I notice.

There is metal.

Metal on the teeth.

Peculiar.

I grip the tongue and pull until it rips loose. I am still hungry, always hungry, but I do not eat it. I save it to take back to the hollow one.

We are full and satisfied, and badly in need of grooming. Some bug-kind have already found us.

Not much meat is left on the other-kind's body, but we gather it as well as we can. The scraps and morsels clinging to the bones, the spleen and lungs, the head that still has face and scalp and delicious brain inside that solid shell of skull.

The cave seems far away. We trudge. Our feet drag. I feel heavy, swollen, satisfied.

Satisfied ... and strange.

Hot. Hot in the pit of my stomach. Hot as if I swallowed the sun whole.

And itchy. The stump of my small-finger, my missing toes, the rim of my ear, the long gash on my hip where the beast-kind gored me ... those spots most of all, but other spots, too, prickle with an intensifying, maddening itch.

The skinny one moans with discomfort. The tall quick one rubs fitfully at some old damage, two holes high on the right side of the torso, below the shoulder.

It takes a long time until we near the cave.

We all feel strange.

We ache. We tingle. We itch.

Something inside my chest clenches in a sudden painful squeeze-thump. I suck in breath with a gasp, let it out with a grunt. The sensation passes. Then squeeze-thumps again. And again.

The cave is not far now.

My mouth is parched. My lips are cracked and dry. I am thirsty, so thirsty.

Thirsty?

The sunlight is a harsh white glare, squinting my eyes, making them water. It burns on my skin, where the marks show in vivid color and design.

There is dampness on me. Under my arms, on my forehead, trickling along my spine. Damp, even under the baking sun-shine, cooler when a breeze gusts. More dampness, thicker and wetter dampness, is in the wounds on my sore hip and calf. I feel it welling up, oozing down. I limp.

The noseless one stands sentry on a high flat boulder. Turned in our direction, alert.

Close now. Very close. The cave is just ahead.

I feel my bowels rumble. I feel pressure in my bladder. My breathing is ragged, raspy. I cough.

The tall quick one whimpers. Blood dribbles from the old damage, the bullet-holes. Then, all at once, the dribbles turn into a flood. The tall quick one takes two more steps, stumbles, falls flat, does not move.

The skinny one cries out for help. But the cry becomes a retching gurgle as the skinny one bends double and vomits up a torrent of partially-chewed meat and organs in a pinkish stew of fluids.

The noseless one must have given a call, because the group is coming.

All of them.

The biggest one, the wobble-headed one, the half-faced one, the tiny shrunken one. Even the hollow one.

They are coming.

Arms raised. Groaning and wailing.

They are hungry.

All, always, very hungry.

And we have returned ... with meat.

BE BRAVE

GERMANY, 194-

Klara didn't want to be on the train.

Mustn't cry. Mustn't whine.

It would be all right. Mutti had promised. Mutti had promised, and Mutti never lied.

But, if Mutti had promised, and Mutti never lied, how come Mutti had tears in her eyes when she said it?

"It will be all right," Mutti had said. "We'll be together again soon, Klara, I promise. You just be brave, my good brave girl, and everything will be fine."

Then Mutti was gone.

Klara wished she could jump out of the crowded car, just jump and run and be away. Nobody would bother trying to stop her, would they? She was only ten, who would care?

Besides, she could run fast.

Or, she could if she left her suitcase.

They'd let her bring a suitcase, just one, stuffed with hastily-packed clothes. If she left it behind on the train, she might never get it back.

Couldn't leave it behind. Couldn't run fast carrying it, having it bump and bang into people. Somebody surely would notice, then.

It was too late, anyway. The doors latched shut. The steam whistle shrieked. The train started moving. It shuddered and jerked as it picked up speed, then settled into a steady rattling kind of rocking motion.

Klara huddled as small in her seat as she could, suitcase between her feet. She held Gerte on her lap, bowing her head over the doll's fluffy curls. Gerte wore a pretty blue dress with lace ruffles. Klara wore a grey traveling coat.

No crying. No whining. Be brave.

Mutti's good brave girl.

Her chin tried to quiver. She made it stop.

It would be fine. They'd be together again soon. Mutti had promised.

But what if something bad happened?

Bad things did happen. It was war-time, and in war-time, bad things always happened. The soldiers. The fighting. The bombings.

What if a bomb hit the train?

Or what if a bomb hit a bridge, and the engineer didn't see it in time?

Her chin tried harder to quiver, and she bit her jaws together so hard they hurt.

She wanted her Mutti. She wanted to be home, in the warm kitchen, with chicken and dumplings cooking on the stove.

What if she never-ever got to go home ever again?

She hugged Gerte tight. She blinked until the stinging in her eyes went away, and gulped silently until the lump in her throat did, too.

Good brave girl.

Taking a deep breath, she lifted her head to glance around. She saw another girl, about her own age, a skinny girl with a snub nose and braids tied in red ribbons. The other girl wore a too-big brown dress that must have been a hand-me-down, and had an old carpet-bag with a scuffed handle.

The other girl looked as scared and alone as Klara felt. When their gazes met, they studied each other for a moment, then mustered their strength long enough to share a brief, shaky smile.

And the train continued its rumbling journey through the countryside.

They thought they could do this? Those bastards, those pig-dogs!

Just come in and oust them from their own land?

Jakob Stumpf would not stand for it.

His family had held and worked this land for over three hundred years.

Tell them they were not true Germans? Tell them they had to leave their home, to make way for some pampered city-bred *Volk* who were more deserving somehow because they were more 'pure'?

It was an outrage.

Jakob Stumpf wished the soldiers who'd come to drive them off had been aggressive about it. Then, they could have fought back ... they could have resisted, done something ...

He'd heard stories of when the Nazis had come to other villages, jeering and mocking, committing random destruction or abuses. He'd heard of young men beaten up for sport, young women shamed, houses looted, barns burned, people robbed.

Why was it just his luck that these ones had been so professional, treating everyone with a brusque but iron-clad respect? Why hadn't they been the cruel monsters that might have inspired his neighbors to action, instead of meek and wretched compliance?

They hadn't burst in on hapless villagers in the night, turning them out of their beds half-wakened and bewildered. Nor was it as if they'd put them to the road with nothing but the clothes on their backs. They'd permitted everyone to gather some personal possessions, keepsakes, even a few valuables before sending them away, telling them not to return.

It was no less an outrage.

This was their land!

Blood and soil, the Party went on about in their speeches.

Blood and soil? How much Stumpf blood had been shed for the sake of this soil? Over three hundred years' worth ... blood and sweat and tears ... bringing crops from the stubborn earth, tending livestock through droughts and bitter winters ...

Jakob had been *born* here, as had his brothers, his father and uncles, his grandfather, his sons! Their ancestors were *buried* here, blood and *bone* and soil!

But, no.

They were not *true* Germans, not *pure* enough. They were descendants of Poles, and Slavs. Perhaps even Jews, generations back. That, in the eyes of the Party, made them mongrels and undesirables.

So, they had to go. They had to go, leave their homes and most of their furnishings behind, leave their animals as property of the fatherland, and therefore property of the *Reich*.

Hans, his own brother, told him to simply accept their fate.

"They are taking our home!" Jakob had said. "Giving it to settlers, to city-dwellers, to spoiled would-be farmers who know nothing of farming, who will ruin everything we've built here."

To that, Hans shrugged. "They let us go with no trouble. We should count ourselves lucky."

Lucky!

Of course, it was Anna that Hans was thinking of, and how easy it would have been for the soldiers to decide Anna was too blonde and too *pure* to be *his* wife.

"They are making our village into a garrison and supply depot," Jakob had persisted. "Stockpiling explosives, weapons, poison gas! And that camp! That *camp* they've built!"

"But what would you have us do?"

"Fight back!"

"Fight back," Hans had echoed, shaking his head.

"We know the land here. We know it better than anyone. We know the woods. We can hide, and strike, and escape, and strike again."

"The two of us, against an army? Against a nation?"

"Others would join us. There are men among our neighbors, our countrymen, who would stand against this ... this tyranny!"

"If we go, we live," Hans said. "Your plan means death, my brother."

With that, Hans had taken his wife, and followed the others. Abandoning the farm that had been their family's lifeblood – blood and bone and soil, blood and sweat and tears – for over three centuries.

But Jakob stayed.

After the train were the trucks, two long trucks, covered in grey-green canvas.

Soldiers took all the bags and suitcases, and threw them into the back of the first one. It was also full of metal barrels, canisters, and crates marked with the swastika flag.

A blond man with the coldest eyes Klara had ever seen reached for Gerte, but another stayed him with a gesture. That one had softer eyes, almost the same blue as Gerte's dress. He patted Klara on the shoulder as she shuffled past. She wondered if he had sisters back home, and missed them.

Her whole life felt further away than she could have imagined. She didn't even know where they were, way out here, surrounded by farms and fields and wooded hills. Where was Mutti right now? Was Mutti thinking of her? Was Mutti sad, though trying to be as brave as she'd urged Klara to be?

Clutching Gerte in one arm, Klara clambered up into the second truck. For seats, they had rough plank benches along the sides, and a double-bench down the middle. She was able to squirm her way past the jostling larger bodies and sit beside the girl with the brown braids. They shared another shaky smile.

Was talking allowed? Klara didn't know, and didn't want to get in trouble, but ...

"I'm Klara," she whispered. "What's your name?"

"Helgie," the girl whispered back. "I like your doll."

"Thank you. She's called Gerte. Would you like to hold her?"

"I better not," said Helgie.

"Maybe later."

They fell quiet, watchful as the rest of the benches filled up. An older girl said something flirty-sounding to the soldiers, who laughed. Then they pulled down the canvas flap at the back and tied it secure, casting the interior into a shadowy gloom.

A few nervous murmurs arose. Klara managed not to join them, but she leaned toward Helgie without pausing to think about it. To her relief, Helgie was doing the same thing, leaning toward her, their arms pressed together.

It helped. It made the dark not so bad. They could still be scared, but it was better to not feel entirely alone. Being brave was easier with a friend.

The truck engines coughed, sputtered, and roared to life. Moments later, they were bouncing along a rutted dirt road. The faster the trucks went, the bumpier the ride became. It was almost fun, at first, with some hoots and cries of alarmed excitement, but soon it was a grueling ordeal of hanging on, so as not to be thrown off the bench.

As the tires juddered across a bridge, the girl who'd flirted with the soldiers announced that she was getting splinters in her you-know-where, which elicited a few snickering giggles. Aside from that, though, the mood soon soured and sombered.

Conversation was next to impossible. The air under the canvas was hot and stuffy, exhaust-smelling and dust-smelling and sweat-smelling, and then even worse-smelling as someone was noisily sick on the floorboards.

Klara closed her eyes and tried to imagine she was on a ship at sea, instead of in this jolting, bouncing truck. On a ship at sea, with her family, all of them safe and happy and on their way to someplace new, someplace where there wasn't war.

Finally, the truck slowed, then turned, then slowed again and came to a wheezing stop. Cab doors creaked open and thumped shut. Boots gritted on gravel. The soldiers untied the flap again. Light flooded in, making everybody squint and wince ... but a fresh breeze flooded in, as well, and they all turned gratefully toward it.

Stiff, sore, and moving like they *all* had splinters in their you-know-wheres, they climbed down. Klara and Helgie went hand-in-hand, having clasped them just as unthinkingly as they'd leaned toward each other on the bench. Helgie shaded her face with her free hand, while Klara held Gerte.

Distant figures labored in garden rows and fields. High wooden gantry-like towers overlooked strange structures that Klara could not identify, where it sounded as if some sort of activity was going on. Long, low barracks or bunkhouses were arranged around a square yard.

The gravel drive that led from the gate widened into a semi-circle in front of a building that resembled a large farm-house.

A woman waited for them on the steps, a tall woman with very pale gold hair pinned back in a bun. She wore a calf-length skirt of dark blue wool, a short-sleeved white blouse with shoulder passants, a black neckerchief, and shiny black shoes with sensible hose.

"I am *Untergau* Wegener," she said. "On behalf of the League of German Girls, I welcome you to Grünfeld School, Farm and Sports Camp."

Jakob Stumpf watched the trucks drive into the heart of the village, raising plumes of dust.

The village. *His* village.

He barely recognized it, now.

Oh, the outlying farmhouses – his own included – were largely the same ... if repaired, renovated, and tidied in preparation for the new families that would arrive soon to take them over.

Those interlopers. Those true, pure Germans.

Good, diligent, hard-working men and women.

As if the people who'd built this place by the strength of their backs and the sweat of their brows hadn't been?

The same old argument, and no one else here to dispute it with him, but it rankled no less.

Jakob supposed that he, too, would be barely recognizable, if seen by anyone who'd known him before. Hiding out in the woods, sleeping in an old hunting-shelter, living on canned food and whatever else he could scrounge ... unshaven, his dark hair long and unkempt ... indifferently bathed ...

He doubtless looked every inch the mongrel their doctrine would have them believe.

Fine. Let them believe it, these clean-cut young men, strutting and proud in their uniforms. He hadn't had much opportunity, yet, but Jakob would make them sorry for what they'd done. For how they'd treated his family and his neighbors, and for what they'd done to his home.

The general store made into a commissary, the tavern into a mess hall, the swastika waving from the flagpole, the church being used as a supply depot ...

The church!

He'd never been the most religious of men, but found this last change the most deeply offensive. The pews had been pushed aside to clear the floorspace, which was now stacked with everything from dynamite to toilet paper.

And to think, less than a hundred yards away, down a grassy slope dotted with wildflowers, was the crumbling stone wall around the tree-shaded cemetery dating back more than three hundred years. His mother, resting there alongside his father and both sets of grandparents, would have wept to see the church she'd loved so much put to such purpose.

The lead truck parked in front of the church. Soldiers began unloading its cargo of crates, metal drums, and heavy canisters painted various colors. The second truck parked by the feed-and-hardware store. It seemed that one held no cargo, but had been used for some other purpose that necessitated being hosed out.

A troop-truck with no troops. A delivery, then. To the camp at what had once been the old Grünfelder farm. The camp for girls.

It wasn't so bad at all!

Oh, at first, Klara was homesick and missed her Mutti, but soon she was too busy to stay sad for long.

There were so many things to do!

Every day, they marched, and recited the pledges, and sang "The Flag on High."

And school, yes, lots of that. History lessons, geography, reading and math, some art, some science, some music. Daily chore rosters were posted, saying who would help in the kitchen or laundry or dining room, who would clean the bathrooms, who would sweep and mop. They worked in the vegetable gardens, orchards, and farm-fields.

On 'Home Evenings', they did housewifely things, like sewing, cooking, handicrafts, planning a budget or menu, and learning how to take care of babies. Saturdays were for 'Outdoor Training', with running, swimming, gymnastics, and sports. The wooden towers Klara had noticed upon arrival were part of an obstacle course, with ropes and ladders, walls to climb, and wires to crawl under.

There were badges that could be earned, as well. They watched instructional films. They studied first aid. They memorized codes and signals. The older girls were taught to drive, and shoot, and take care of weapons. They were also lectured regularly on *rassenschande*, which, as Klara and Helgie understood it, had to do with having the wrong kinds of boyfriends.

The two of them were the youngest at Grünfeld, but there were a few others who were eleven and twelve. Most of the rest were between thirteen and sixteen, with some seventeen-and-olders who served more as teachers and assistants.

It was like having many big sisters, none of whom were mean or spiteful. Well, except for Inge, sometimes. Inge often said how she had joined the League expecting that she'd meet and marry a handsome SS officer, not be put in charge of a bunch of little girls. Whenever she complained, Marlene – the one who'd flirted with the soldiers as she boarded the truck, and who still did whenever she had the opportunity – would just laugh.

Each girl was expected to make her own bed, and keep herself and her belongings tidy. They all had uniforms very like the one *Untergau* Wegener had been wearing when she greeted them: white blouses, dark blue skirts, black neckerchiefs and shoes, but instead of hose they wore cuffed white socks.

The food wasn't quite as good as Mutti made at home, but it was healthy and there was always plenty of it. More sweets would have been nice, but those were saved for special occasions and extra rewards. Other rewards included being allowed to go horseback riding, or stay up past lights-out, or listen to the radio.

To think, she'd been upset about going away to summer camp! To think, she'd almost cried, and Mutti had to tell her to be brave, her good brave girl, hugging her and promising that it'd be all right. She'd been worried about being alone, and now she had dozens of new friends and big sisters.

Most of all, she had a new very-best friend in Helgie. Who was really Helgemunde, for her grandmother, but who'd want to be called Helgemunde all the time? Ugh. Helgie was here because her mother and father both worked double shifts in the factories most of the time, and got a subsidy to help afford sending her to camp.

Untergau Wegener could be stern and strict, but she could also be nice. She wanted them to grow up to become the kind of fine, strong, self-reliant young women who would be a credit to their families, their country, and their heritage. They had a responsibility, she told them. A great and important responsibility to the future.

Also, she carried packets of lemon drops, and would hand them out as treats.

The time had come. He could endure no more of it.

No more of the soldiers, going around as if they owned the village. No more of the 'true' German families brought from the cities to take over the farms. No more of the Hitler Youth girls that the camp sent to help educate them.

No more. Just no more.

Jakob had hoped they'd give up, abandon this plan, and go away. He'd known it a vain hope, but he'd hoped it all the same.

His efforts to discourage them had little effect, or were dismissed as accidents. What could a single man do against so many, without being discovered?

He dreamed of picking them off one by one, taking them by surprise, overpowering them, throttling them, crushing in their skulls with heavy stones, throwing their bodies into gullies layered deep with decades' worth of fallen leaves.

But the soldiers were armed and alert, diligent in their duties, for all that they were far from any active battlefield or front.

Then he'd hoped that Hans, and his uncles, and others of their displaced neighbors, would see the error of their ways. They would return, and join him in reclaiming their land, their homes.

That hope, as well, proved to be in vain.

Better, he finally decided, that it all be destroyed.

And was there any way more fitting, than to do it by using their own weapons against them?

Jakob waited all night in the woods, readying himself, mustering his nerve.

Just before dawn, he crept through the cemetery. He paused only long enough at the graves of his parents and grandparents to beg their forgiveness for what he was about to do, though he was certain they understood.

At the back of the church, all but obscured by weeds, piled junk, and old lumber was a warped wooden door set into the banked earth, at an angle. The Nazis either hadn't noticed it, or deemed it not worth bothering with.

The door, once uncovered, pulled open with a rusty groan. He descended into dank, cobwebby darkness that smelled of mildew, vinegar, and decay. A flickering match let him pick his way through a warren of discarded furniture, shelves of books and hymnals swollen fat from the damp, and sprung rat-traps pinning carcasses like twisted rags of matted fur.

He paused at the foot of the stairs, listened, heard nothing, and proceeded up. The steps creaked, and he realized he might have a problem if they'd thought to install a new bolt on the other side.

They hadn't.

Jakob shook out the match, able to rely now on the pale morning light coming in through the tall, narrow eastern windows. Instead of pews, it shone on stacked crates, barrels, boxes, drums, and metal canisters. Some of the words on the labels were strings of chemical-sounding words that made no sense to him. Others – oil, grease, solvent – brought a grim smile to his bearded, dirty face.

When he and Hans had been boys, their father took them along to help a neighbor blast a stubborn boulder out of his field. Their Uncle Franz hadn't been a farmer, but worked the mines and quarries, and would talk for hours over his beer.

Those experiences, and stories, might not have made Jakob an expert on dynamite. But, he reasoned, he knew enough to get the job done.

***

Eggs, toast, and porridge with raisins filling their stomachs, the girls of Grünfeld camp went about their morning chores and exercises beneath a pink-streaked silvery-blue sky.

Birds twittered in the treetops, fieldmice scampered in the grass, a deer grazed daintily by the orchard fence, and ducks paddled across the lake.

Then came the explosion.

Like a thunderclap and a landslide and a roaring train and a bomb blast, all in one.

The ground trembled briefly underfoot.

After an instant's shocked silence, all the birds launched themselves in wheeling mad flutters up and away. The ducks, too, flapping faster and faster to lift from the water. The deer vanished in springing bounds.

The younger girls were in the vegetable garden when it happened. They all turned as one. So did the girls supervising them, and the ones who'd been going for a health-run, and everybody else.

Windows opened. Heads popped out. Girls rushed from the kitchen, dishrags in hand, soap-suds to their elbows. In the stable, girls tried to soothe startled horses. In the barn, girls yelped as cows kicked over their milk-pails.

More explosions followed, smaller ones, milder, an irregular stuttering fusillade. Like firecrackers, like pine knots in a campfire, like popcorn or chestnuts, *pow-boom-kabang*.

Untergau Wegener burst through the front door and onto the porch, two teachers with her, all of them holding guns.

They looked north, in the direction of the village.

It was about two miles away by the dirt road, but much less than that on a path that cut through the woods and over the footbridge that spanned a chuckling creek.

As part of their service, the girls went there to help the new families settling in, and to cheer the community by organizing choir concerts and parties. That was always great fun and they all enjoyed it ... especially the older girls, like Marlene, who got to dance with the garrison's soldiers.

Now there was a big fuming cloud of smoke rising over the trees. A billowy grey-black column, sooty and gritty-looking, but also tinged a nasty yellowish-green. Flames wavered in it. Sparks whirled. Something else blew up with a loud hollow *buwhoom*.

A bell clanged urgent summons, the stark iron bell on the porch. *Untergau* Wegener began barking orders.

Everyone raced to obey. Older girls herded younger ones toward the house. Within minutes, they had gathered in the dining room, the only room large enough to hold them all at once. The tables were only half-cleared from breakfast, and brooms leaned against the walls.

A babble of nervous voices – were they being bombed? was it the Americans? – cut off when *Untergau* Wegener came in. She told them that, as far as she knew, no, they were not under attack, they were not being bombed, no British or American planes had been spotted nearby.

Her best guess was that there'd been a mishap at the supply depot ... or perhaps sabotage. For now, they would stay put, stay inside, and stay calm.

"Be brave," Klara whispered to Helgie, who nodded, chewing on the end of a braid.

"Trudi and Lisbeth are riding to the village to see what's going on," *Untergau* Wegener continued. "Nora will be organizing volunteers of ages fifteen and older for sentry and watch duty. Everyone else, finish your house-chores and then you may read, study, or socialize quietly among yourselves until we have more information. Yes?"

"Yes, *Untergau* Wegener," they replied in unison.

She gave a satisfied nod. Her cool blue gaze moved over them in thoughtful evaluation. She hesitated, pressing her lips into a tight line, and glanced toward the windows in the north wall.

The smoke-cloud had flattened and spread, that nasty yellow-green color making the sky look the way being sick felt. They'd learned about mustard gas and phosgene and other horrors in their lessons; some of the girls here had aunts or sisters in the League who'd had to be given gas masks when they went to help settlers in a place called Hegewald.

Untergau Wegener drew a sharp breath and nodded again, decisively. She added, "Those of you who've earned marksmanship badges, please accompany me to my office."

Jakob sat up, pushing aside chunks of debris.

His head felt stuffed with cotton and buzzing, drilling brass bees. He couldn't hear anything past that buzz. He couldn't feel anything but numbness, even as he *saw* himself moving, even as he *knew* that he was not paralyzed.

He had expected a noise, some fire.

This ...

Where the church had been ...

Split timbers and pieces of masonry jutted at odd angles from blazing rubble that seemed simultaneously piled and caved in. Bricks, shingles, burning embers, and shards of glass had sprayed everywhere. Some still rained down; he saw it thudding down all around him, though he could neither feel nor hear it.

Smoke and flame churned high. More metal drums burst like bombs, showering fuel in a fiery rain.

In the village, soldiers ran back and forth. Jakob presumed they were shouting, but he couldn't hear that, either. The blast had deafened him, as well as slapping him halfway across the cemetery, with its concussive force.

He saw sprawled bodies, clothes scorched, skin blackened, motionless. He saw people – the interloping would-be farmers, as well as soldiers – limping, bleeding, wounded. Women sobbed and children wailed, but Jakob still could not hear.

Sensation began to return to him, a tingling of pins and needles. He worked faster to uncover his legs. He should have been well away into the woods by now, hiding. If they found him, they'd shoot him. He was sure of it.

More smoke, sickly-colored vapors, did not so much waft out of the wreckage as seethe from it, seeping low and thick and heavy, rolling over the contours of the ground like a slow wind, or current of cloudy water.

The shrill buzzing in his ears and head faded into a rushing sort of echo. It occurred to him that the sickly-colored smoke, flowing downhill, bending the grass and wildflowers before it, was headed toward him.

Hadn't he said something to Hans about poison gas? Those canisters, the ones labeled with such incomprehensible strings of words, what had been in them? What had been released when they ruptured? What was in that unholy mixture of chemicals now coursing steadily this way? The stories from the front, the images in the newspapers ... hideous agony and blisters, the flesh sloughing off limbs like melting wax ...

The gas reached the old stone wall. It permeated the cracks. Dammed, it deepened and built up until it spilled over, then flooded out among the tombstones, spreading, sinking.

Movement in the fog caught his eye. A rat, he saw, struggling clumsily, almost dragging itself by the forepaws with its head hunched to the side. A scrawny thing, little more than fur and bones ...

Fur in shedding patches, mangy, matted ... bones showing through it ... poking and splintered. It couldn't be alive, hurt so badly. Why, even its eyes were gone, blinded sunken sockets.

He saw another, trap still clamped to its broken neck, hitching along with a grotesque humping gait.

The rats couldn't be alive? No, they couldn't, and they weren't. He remembered the carcasses he'd seen in the church cellar –

Jakob managed to get to his feet before the encroaching greenish tendrils reached him. He took a single step, tripped over a tombstone, and fell headlong into the gas. He flinched in anticipation of soul-rending pain –

That wasn't.

The gas didn't sting, didn't burn, didn't feel like anything but a chilly miasma coating his skin.

Nor did it reek of mustard, chlorine, or other violent stinks. It smelled ... almost sweet ... he thought of his grandmother making doughnuts ...

He pushed himself to his hands and knees, breaching out of the layer of murky gas. Wisps of it ran down his arms. He coughed.

The first rat, the one with its head lolling, bit him on the wrist. *That*, he felt. Blood trickled down his hand.

Then the earth around him, the earth covering the graves of his parents and grandparents and ancestors dating back three hundred years, quivered and upheaved.

The dark soil crumbled as bony fingers thrust up through it.

The horses returned at a gallop, each burdened with a passenger, in addition to Trudi and Lizbeth. The passengers were soldiers, one unconscious, the other clinging weakly to Lizbeth, both with their uniforms blood-stained.

Girls ran for stretchers and first aid kits from the nurse's office. They moved tables to clear space in the dining room and set up cots. The ones *Untergau* Wegener had armed went to join Nora's sentries on watch, alert.

In the hectic moments that followed, Klara recognized the second soldier as the same one who'd patted her on the shoulder as she'd moved toward the truck.

Marlene knew him. His name was Erich, she said, Erich Löwe. The other was Glaussen, she thought.

Erich Löwe was white-faced with shock, babbling.

"... the gas ... the dead ... keep getting up ... shot them, had to ... shot Mertz and Bauman ... the cows the dogs the rats, them, too, it's in them ... the head, got to ... the head, the brain ... look out for the gas ... coming ... hungry ... Ritter torn apart, torn to pieces ... had to shoot Mertz, would have killed us, tried to kill Glaussen ... bit ..."

Then he, too, fell into unconsciousness.

Trudi and Lizbeth, meanwhile, spoke in overlapping staccato as they made their reports to *Untergau* Wegener. They'd gotten close enough to the village to see that apparently the church – being used as a supply depot – had exploded and burned, the fire spreading to engulf other buildings.

"—injured or dead --"

"—people everywhere, even animals --"

"—complete panic and disaster --"

"—smoke, and the gas --"

"—strange fog, low, not rising but spreading along the ground --"

"—didn't think we should get any closer --"

As they'd been trying to decide what to do next, they'd encountered Löwe and Glaussen stumbling down the trail, wounded and coughing. So, they'd hauled the soldiers onto their horses and ridden back as fast as they could.

Untergau Wegener snapped her girls to attention and began issuing brisk orders. The gas masks were to be brought down from the attic, more first aid kits and medical supplies gathered, same for relief packets of water and emergency rations, the horses moved to the barn in case they needed to convert the stable to a field hospital, and so on.

They sprang into action. The younger girls helped fetch and carry boxes and bottles and folded sheets. Klara, remembering Löwe's previous kindness, brought Gerte from the shelf above her bed and set the doll beside him on the cot.

The nurse turned from Glaussen, shook her head at *Untergau* Wegener, and drew a sheet over the soldier's head. It settled onto him.

"Nerve gas?" asked *Untergau* Wegener.

"Hard to say. He also lost a great deal of blood."

"He was shot?"

"No. Cut, maybe stabbed? I would almost say he was bitten by animals."

"And the other one? Löwe?"

"Uninjured. The blood is from other sources. He has no gas burns or blisters on his skin, but whatever he inhaled ... it would help if we knew what they'd been storing."

A flurry of alarmed cries interrupted whatever the *Untergau* had been about to reply. Lizbeth, coming back from the barn, had collapsed on the porch, where she twitched and convulsed.

"She's having a seizure!" The nurse ran out there. "The gas, she must have been exposed! Where's Trudi?"

"The horses!" someone cried from the direction of the barn. "The horses are sick! They're fighting! Attacking each other, and the cows! It's like they've gone mad!"

"Masks on," *Untergau* Wegener commanded. "Everyone who's had contact with the horses or these men, wash your --"

"*Untergau* Wegener?" ventured Helgie, in a very worried voice. "Should he be getting up?"

Klara looked at Löwe, but Löwe was motionless except for the faint stirrings of shallow breaths.

On the other cot, the sheet covering Glaussen slid away as he sat up. He moved with jerky, awkward motions, shifting his legs over the side.

"But he's dead," Marlene said.

Groaning, he tottered to his feet. He did *look* dead, his features slack, his eyes half-lidded murky marbles.

"Stand back, girls," *Untergau* Wegener said.

Glaussen took a lurching, staggering step. The *Untergau* extended an arm, setting the heel of her hand to his chest to stop his advance.

"That's far enough, soldier --" she began.

He grasped her wrist, pulled, and sank his teeth into the meaty part of her forearm, like a man biting into a chicken leg. Blood squirted. Girls screamed.

Untergau Wegener hissed with pain. She drove forward, hard, slamming the man against the wall, pinning him there with her arm braced solidly in his gnawing, chewing mouth. With her other hand she snatched the pistol from her belt. She jammed the barrel between his eyes and blew out the back of his head in jellied clots of brain, bone, and hair.

He dropped at once and did not move again.

More screams and cries erupted outside. The girls who'd been standing watch started shouting that people were approaching, coming across the north field, and that some kind of smoke or gas was blowing this way, as well.

"Masks!" repeated the *Untergau*. She ripped the sleeve off her own blouse, bandaged her savaged arm, and tied her neckerchief as a tourniquet. "Masks *now*, girls! Masks and weapons!"

True and pure Germans? Poles, Slavs, Jews? Mongrels?

It no longer mattered.

The freshly killed corpses of soldiers and settlers trudged clumsily alongside the cadaverous, rotted, or skeletal remains of villagers who'd clawed their way up from their graves.

Jakob Stumpf, or the thing that had once been Jakob Stumpf, went with them. So did the rats from the church basement's traps, and livestock, and stray dogs.

Human or animal, that no longer mattered, either.

They were united, of one nation and one heritage. Driven by their one common purpose, by their shared goal.

Ahead, at the camp, they would feed.

If the gas got them, they died.

They died and they came back, and then they killed.

Like the soldier, Glaussen.

Like the horses, and Lizbeth, and Trudi.

And the other soldier, Erich Löwe?

His eyes opened. Soft blue eyes, almost the same color as Gerte's dress. They opened and he looked at Klara, though her face was hidden by heavy rubber, canvas, and leather.

Her little hand patted him on the shoulder. She picked up the pistol that *Untergau* Wegener had set down in order to bandage her arm. She held it to his ear. He smiled his gratitude.

Klara smiled back. Then she pulled the trigger.

After that, she went to join the rest. Those that were left.

They waited, girls aged ten to seventeen. Girls in dark blue skirts, white blouses, black neckerchiefs, and gas masks. Some armed with guns, others with farm tools or sports equipment.

"Ready?" asked the *Untergau,* a Mauser M712 *Schnellfeuer* cradled over her wounded arm.

"Ready," they said.

Ready to make a stand. To fight, and defend their country, and make their families proud. Ready to be brave.

FAMILY LIFE

"KIDS, DINNER'S READY," I called.

Grampy was already there, slouched in his usual spot at the end of the table. His teeth were beside his plate. Drool ran from his slack lips. I saw his tongue sliding over his puffy gums in anticipation. He garbled something interrogative at me.

I hadn't been able to understand my father-in-law when he was alive. Nowadays, it was hopeless.

"What, Grampy?"

He rolled his eyes. They, like his teeth, were beside his plate. His spidery, bony fingers toyed with the murky orbs. They leaked a little, leaving snail-trails on the tablecloth. He made the questioning mumble again.

Caitlin had entered the dining room in time to hear him, despite the headphones clamped to her ears. "He asked what's for dinner," she said, with the haughtiness that only a teenager could master.

"Take those things off," I said, indicating the headphones.

She rolled her eyes, too, but at least Caitlin's were still in their sockets. As she obeyed, I heard the perky percussive slam-bounce of the music. Life-metal. Typical. Kids had to rebel. When I was her age, the edgy your-parents-will-hate-it music was all about death and darkness and nihilism.

Davey came in from the backyard, so filthy he might have just clawed his way out of a muddy grave. I took one look and sent him straight to the sink to wash up.

"Aw, Mom!"

"Don't 'aw, Mom' me, mister. Where's Tess?"

In answer, I felt a small hand plucking at my skirt. I looked down at my youngest, my baby. Tess was dragging her stuffed rabbit by one tattered ear and had a thumb in her mouth.

"Where did you get that?" I asked, removing it. "Is this your father's thumb?"

Tess wrinkled up her face and started to whimper. I relented, returning it to her. If it was Stuart's thumb, he had no one to blame but himself for leaving it lying around. In almost twenty years of marriage, I hadn't been able to break him of the habit of leaving his dirty socks all over the place, let alone body parts. Tess bit down happily, gnawing at the thick ivory-yellow nail. She only had six teeth, but that still put her ahead of Grampy. I lifted her into her booster chair.

"Okay?" asked Davey, presenting his hands for my inspection. They were grey-green, the skin peeling, the scabs on his knuckles worn away to reveal bare bone, but they were clean.

"Good enough," I said.

As I was dishing up the meal, Stuart arrived with his briefcase. His tie, and the loose hanging flesh of his neck and trachea, were pulled askew at the collar. He gave me a perfunctory kiss on the cheek, greeted his father, sat down, and buried his nose in the newspaper. I saw that he was missing his right pinkie finger and half his index finger, but had both thumbs. Tess must have picked up her chew-toy outside. There were plenty of bits and pieces around the neighborhood, and that was just the way it was with a child as small as Tess. Anything she could pick up went right into her mouth. Marbles, pennies, bugs, dead mice … in it went.

"Brainloaf again?" groaned Davey as I set his plate before him. "We just *had* brainloaf."

"Moth-errrr!" Caitlin repeated the eye-roll. "How many times do I have to tell you? I don't eat that stuff anymore."

"Caitlin, don't be silly," I said. "Eat your brain. It's good for you."

"I'm a vegetarian, remember?"

Stuart lowered his paper and peered at her. "Since when?"

"Since I decided it's cruel and inhumane to prey upon living creatures," she said. "If you listened, if anybody in this family cared about my feelings –"

"We could have Brain Helper," Davey suggested, poking without enthusiasm at the steaming pink-brown slab. "I like Brain Helper."

"We're having this," I said.

"What do you mean, cruel and inhumane?" Stuart asked Caitlin. "How do you expect to survive?"

"We don't *need* to eat brains! There are alternatives!"

"Like cauliflower?" Davey snickered. "That at least *looks* like a brain."

"Shut up, Davey."

"Make me!"

"I've about had enough out of you, young lady," Stuart said. "First that horrible music, and the way you dress, and now this!"

"What's wrong with the way I dress?"

"Look at you! Susan, help me out here."

I finished mashing Grampy's brainloaf into a lumpy paste that he could spoon up, and moved on to cutting a slice into manageable pieces for Tess. "Well, Caitlin, your father does have a point. That pink makeup ..."

"I like it. Don't I have a right to express my individuality?"

"If all the kids are doing it, what's individual about that?" Stuart asked.

"I knew you wouldn't understand!" She pushed back from the table so hard that the splintery white end of her ulna jabbed out through her forearm. "Oh, great! See what you made me do?"

"You get back here and eat your dinner, young lady!" Stuart shouted after her as she stormed out.

"Stu, let her go," I said.

"Are you going to let her do this to herself?"

"She'll eat when she's hungry."

"But she's already just skin and bones."

I shrugged. "It's not like she'll starve to death."

The rest of us ate our dinner. I saved Caitlin's plate in the fridge for her, in case she changed her mind, but I didn't hold out much hope. Teenagers could be so stubborn. I could always send a cold brainloaf sandwich to work in Stuart's lunch, if he could be persuaded to brown-bag it instead of going out hunting downtown with his colleagues. Or, if there were enough leftovers, maybe Davey would get his way tomorrow night. I still had a box or two of Brain Helper in the cupboard.

Some things, even after the end of the world, never did change.

Here we were, all of us, still going about our daily domestic routines. Stuart went to the office. I took care of the house and the kids. Davey and Caitlin went to school and spent time with their friends. Tess toddled and played. Grampy mumbled about how much better it had been in the good old days.

"So, how was work?" I asked, trying to coax Tess into drinking her bile from a big-girl sippy cup instead of a bottle.

"Mr. Harris wants me to take over Don Foster's job."

"Really? Honey, that's wonderful. But what happened to Don?"

"Shot in the head while walking to his car."

"*Here*? In *our* neighborhood?"

Stu nodded.

I glanced at Davey, hoping he wouldn't be paying attention to boring grown-up talk. But, of course, he was listening avidly.

"I'm sure it must have been an accident," I said. What we'll do to try and protect our children from the ugly truth ...

Of course, it wasn't like Davey hadn't seen his share of ugliness. We all had. I had been right there when one of Caitlin's teachers took a shotgun blast to the face while trying to haul someone out of a truck. Her head had blown apart in a curdled spray, spattering me with cold, sticky gobs. All three of the kids had seen Mr. Algers, the postman, stalking down our street in stiff, jittery strides after someone had buried a hatchet haft-deep in the top of his skull. He had made it as far as our driveway before collapsing.

And then there was what had happened to Rex ...

"Hope they get the one who did it," Stuart said. "Get him and eat him up, struggling and raw, like we used to. Remember that, Davey-boy?"

"Yeah," Davey said. "Can we go hunting this weekend, Dad? Can we?"

"We'll see."

"Oh, Stu, I don't know if that's a good idea," I said. "Davey's so young –"

"You can't treat him like a child forever, Susan."

He was wrong about that – they would *be* children forever – but I didn't want to argue at the dinner table.

"I'll make a casserole for Helen Foster," I said, by way of changing the subject. "It won't be easy for her without Don."

Shot in the head. It was the only way to really be finished, of course. The zombie's worst nightmare. I was always worried that it would happen to Stu, and I'd be left alone with the kids and Grampy to take care of.

The ones I couldn't understand were the live ones who, when backed into a corner, put their own guns to their heads to make sure they wouldn't come back. They acted like it was a fate worse than death.

Like it was so terrible.

A person could get used to about anything, with enough time and a little practice.

All right, maybe it had been a little crazy there near the beginning. Everyone had gone kind of nuts then, living or dead. Riots. Massacres. Armed survivalists. Cities in flames. Martial law. Pockets of resistance. Shambling hoards. Chasing down screaming people and tearing hot, wet chunks out of them ...

Things were better now. Almost back to normal. After all, we still had the things that mattered. We had each other. We had home, and family. Millions of others hadn't been so lucky.

After dinner, Stuart unstrapped Grampy from his chair and carried him into the living room to watch television. Not that there was much on these days that any of us cared to watch. The reruns were all painful reminders from before, and there just wasn't a lot in terms of programming aimed at the new demographic.

I sent Davey up to do his homework, and took Tess in for her bath. I could hear music from Caitlin's room. She was in there, sulking, with the door shut. Probably on the phone with one of her friends.

"Who's a clean girl?" I crooned as I washed Tess. I did it gently, so as not to rub off more than I had to, but as careful as I was, the water soon became filmed with a greasy residue and shed scraps of skin.

Tess giggled and kicked and splashed. I poured baby shampoo into my cupped palm and lathered her fine blonde hair. Some suds ran down her face and into her eyes, but she didn't cry. Just as she never cried whenever I accidentally poked her with a diaper pin.

I dried her off and got her into a set of fuzzy yellow sleepers patterned with duckies. Combing her hair, I struck a tangle and pulled too hard without thinking. A patch of scalp the size of a quarter peeled away from her skull.

"Oh, look at that," I said. "Sorry, sweetie. Mommy's clumsy today."

Davey had finished his homework by the time I carried Tess into their room. He was in his pajamas and had toys spread all over the floor.

"Mom, can I have a puppy?" he asked, looking up as I came in.

"No, dear, you should have eaten all of your dinner."

"I meant as a pet."

"Oh." I sat in the rocker, Tess cradled on my lap. "I don't think so, Davey."

"It wouldn't be like with Rex, I promise. We could get a real puppy. One like us."

"Animals aren't like us, Davey. You know that."

His lower lip stuck out. It was hanging by a flap and would probably fall off any day now. "Why aren't they?"

"Nobody knows," I said, beginning to rock. "They just aren't."

"I miss Rex. I didn't know he wouldn't come back. I was just hungry."

"I know." I smiled at him, my soothing-mommy smile. "I know, honey. Now, go brush your teeth and get into bed. We've got a story to finish."

"Okay." He shuffled off.

As I rocked, I let my gaze roam the kids' bedroom. There was still a family photograph hanging on the wall. I had taken down and gotten rid of all the others, the framed pictures and the albums, but this one I kept forgetting.

I was surprised it didn't give Davey nightmares. Those faces ... faces that were almost familiar. ... faces that were alive ...

To think, that used to be my family.

Davey came back upset, with two teeth in his hand. He showed them to me as if afraid I might scold. "I was just brushing and they came out."

"That's all right. It happens." Tess had drifted off, and I lowered her into her crib. I smoothed the blanket tight over her bloated little tummy and tucked Mr. Bun-Bun down beside her. "Into bed with you."

Once he was in, I returned to the rocker and picked up a thick book from the bedside table. I flipped the colorful pages.

"Do you remember where we left off?" I asked.

"The big brain!" he said, bouncing on the mattress where he had originally died. "The big brain and the zombie godmother!"

I began to read, editing as I went.

***

The zombie godmother waved her magic bone, and the brain that Zombiella had brought from the kitchen grew into a carriage, with six giant graveyard rats for horses.

"Now you can go to the ball," she said.

"But, Godmother!" Zombiella looked down at herself. "How can I go to the ball like this?"

The zombie godmother waved her bone again, and something wonderful happened. Zombiella's soft pink skin turned dark with decay. Her cheeks sank in. Her glossy hair went stringy and dry. The smell of rotting meat rose around her like perfume. The ugly, raggedy clothes that Zombiella's stepsisters made her wear turned into a long white shroud, with slippers carved from skulls, and hairpins made from fingerbones.

"But be home by midnight," the zombie godmother warned, "because at the stroke of twelve, the spell ends."

Zombiella promised to be back in time. She climbed into the brain carriage, and off she went to the ball.

Prince Zombing's castle was all aglow, and there was music, and a tremendous feast of fresh brains, and every zombie girl in the kingdom had come in hopes of being the one the prince chose to be his bride.

But when Zombiella walked in, Prince Zombing's eyes popped right out of his head. Nobody recognized the beautiful green stranger in the long shroud and skull slippers. Not even Zombiella's own jealous stepsisters and cruel stepmother.

Prince Zombing, once he put his eyes back in, would dance with no one else for the rest of the night. They were having such a wonderful time that, before Zombiella knew it, the great clock began to strike twelve. She ran for the exit, and in her hurry, she tripped on the staircase. Her anklebones snapped, and one of her feet, still clad in its skull slipper, broke off. She couldn't go back for it but had to hobble along on the stump until she got back to her brain carriage and the graveyard rats galloped away.

The last stroke of midnight echoed across the land, and the spell ended. The fine carriage turned back to a brain, the rats shrank to their normal size, and Zombiella's shroud became dismal rags. Her heart started beating. Her skin tingled. She was alive again, horribly alive. Blood poured from the stump of her ankle.

On her one remaining foot, though, was a single skull slipper. Zombiella put it in her pocket and limped the rest of the way home.

She was just in time; her cruel stepmother and jealous stepsisters arrived, furious at the mysterious, nameless stranger who had so enchanted the prince. Zombiella smiled to herself and kept quiet, her skull slipper hidden safely away and wrapped up her stump in a big bundle of rags, so no one would guess the truth.

Meanwhile, at the castle, Prince Zombing had found the severed foot on the stairs and swore that he would only marry the zombie girl whose foot it was. He sent his steward from house to house, carrying the foot on a velvet pillow, searching among every girl in the kingdom for its rightful owner.

Well, when Zombiella's stepmother and stepsisters heard about this, they made a plan. The elder stepsister declared that she should get to try first, and as soon as the steward neared their house, she lopped off one of her feet with a cleaver. When he came to the door, she met him, hopping on one leg. The steward was overjoyed to have found the prince's true love, but as soon as he tried to match the foot to the stump, he realized he had been tricked. You see, the foot on the pillow was a *right* foot, and the elder stepsister had foolishly cut off her *left* foot.

The steward was angry, but the second stepsister quickly chopped off *her* foot and hobbled out. So the steward tried again ... but the second stepsister was so eager and excited that she'd cut crooked, leaving most of her heel on. It was obvious that the foot wouldn't match her stump, either.

Really furious now, the steward was about to leave when Zombiella rushed forward and begged to be allowed to try.

"You?" her stepmother cried. "You, a living girl? Don't be ridiculous! The prince would never marry the likes of you!"

"Please, sir," Zombiella said to the steward.

"My orders did say *every* girl ..."

Zombiella sat down and unwrapped her stump. She extended her leg, which ended in an ankle-stump that everyone could see looked like a match ... except that her leg was pink and firm and alive, while the foot on the pillow was green and smelly, its zombie toes twitching.

The steward touched the foot to the stump, and it was a perfect fit. The rot spread quickly up Zombiella's leg and, in seconds, she was revealed to be the mysterious zombie girl that the prince had fallen in love with.

But the cruel stepmother, understanding everything, knocked the steward away. She grabbed the foot, wrenched it off of Zombiella's ankle, and threw it in the fire. It went up in a sizzle of grease and smoke, leaving only the blackened skull slipper.

"You'll never prove it now!" she screamed in triumph.

As the steward was staring in horror at the burnt foot bones and wondering how in the world he would explain to the prince, Zombiella reached into her pocket and brought out the other, matching, skull slipper.

"Well," Zombiella said, "I do have this, the other slipper."

That was all the proof anyone could need, so Zombiella married Prince Zombing and they existed happily ever after.

Davey had gone all drowsy-eyed, but he struggled to stay awake. "Read another one, Mom."

"Tomorrow night."

"Pleeeeeease?"

"Tomorrow night," I repeated firmly.

"Which one?"

I flipped another page. "How about Brainsel and Deadel?"

"Yeah! With the scary live witch and the house made of brains?"

"That's the one."

"And they find their way through the woods by dropping --?"

"Sounds like we don't need to read it if you know the whole story already."

"No, I want to!"

I closed the book and leaned over to give Davey a kiss. "All right, then. Good night, Davey."

"Good night, Mom."

He snuggled down in his bed and closed his eyes. I checked on Tess one last time. She was sleeping like the dead, not breathing, not moving, her little face peaceful, the thumb stuck securely in her mouth.

Leaving the kids' door ajar in case they woke in the night, I stood for a moment in the dim hall. The house was quiet. I could faintly hear the television downstairs, and Stu's occasional gargling chuckles. Maybe a rerun of *Fear Factor;* watching the squeamish living munch on cow eyeballs and rancid fish always amused him.

Caitlin's door was closed, but there was a line of light beneath it. I rapped twice.

"What?"

"It's Mom."

"I told you, I'm not eating that stuff."

I opened the door. Her room was wallpapered in posters of actors and singing idols, a shrine to the hunks and hotties of a dead-and-gone world. Caitlin was sprawled on the rug with a pile of fashion magazines. Stu was right, she *was* skin and bones. Her efforts with makeup might have hidden her greenish pallor, but I knew from personal experience that cosmetics could only do so much.

"You don't have to, if you don't want to," I said.

"Tell that to Dad."

"He's worried about you, that's all. So am I. We just want you to be happy."

"Like anybody really cares."

"I care."

"No, you don't."

"I know this is hard for you, honey. Nobody ever expected things to turn out this way. It's not what you wanted. Believe me, it's not what your father and I wanted for you. But it's what we have. It's what is. We all have to do the best we can to get along. At least we're all still together."

"So what?"

"So what?" I echoed. "So what, Caitlin? I'll tell you so what. We still have each other. We're still a family. That is the most important thing in the world."

"Yeah." She rolled over, away from me, her bones making a brittle rattling noise. "Whatever."

"Someday, maybe you'll understand how much you, and your father, and your brother and sister really mean to me," I said.

"Give it *up*, Mom," she said. "We're dead. It doesn't matter."

"Caitlin –"

She clapped her headphones into place and turned the music back on, cranking it up loud.

I sighed. "When you're ready," I said, doubting that she would answer, even if she could hear me, "we'll talk."

Teenagers. And Caitlin was going to be one forever.

I went into the room I shared with Stuart and sat down at my dressing table. The lights around the mirror showed my reflection with unflattering harshness. The waxy, mossy complexion. The patchy hair that clung to my skull like a bad wig. It had to go. The hairstyle didn't suit me.

The festering scalp was glued in place by a clammy, gelatinous seal of half-dried blood and fluid. I peeled it away. It made a wet slurping noise as it parted company with my head. Grimacing, I dropped the wad of hair and skin onto the floor. It lay there in a heap, looking like roadkill.

Where it had been, my own hair was sweat-damp and matted down. I worked my fingers into it, scratching, not caring that the green greasepaint on my fingers was rubbing off. I needed to redo my makeup anyway.

There was a pot of cold cream on the dressing table. I dunked a cloth into it and began scrubbing in slow circles over my cheeks, chin, and brow. Hatefully healthy pink skin emerged.

Cosmetics could only do so much.

No amount of makeup, no matter how skillfully applied, was going to hide the truth much longer. I could douse myself in Charnel No. 5 from now until forever, but the slaughterhouse stench couldn't conceal the fact that my limbs were whole, my flesh solid, my organs inside where they had always been.

Maybe if I lopped off a finger or two? Knocked out some teeth? Gouged out an eye? Or even take the big step, the final step?

Whatever I did, I knew I had to do it soon. Some of the neighbors had already been getting suspicious. Look at Don Foster, the nosy bastard. I'd hated having to shoot him, but what if he'd said something to Helen? How could I ever show my face in the supermarket again? What if the cruel gossip got back to the kids, somehow?

I finished removing my makeup and changed into my nightgown. It was a skimpy little Victoria's Secret number, lace and wisps of see-through silk, revealing almost everything. All that smooth, firm flesh ...

It was a good thing Stu had always been a bit on the kinky side.

A TOWER TO THE SKY

In the lands between the rivers
Lands rich with silt and clay
Where the fields of barley grow
Where sheep and oxen lay
Will a ziggurat be built
Five-thousand cubits high
The jewel of Babylonia
A tower to the sky

Rilah plucked at the lyre's strings as she sang, her sweet voice drifting over the camp.

No one else paid much attention.

Jehal would have liked to pay more attention, much more. To stop and listen, to smile at her ... to hopefully elicit a smile in return, or at least a glance from beneath those long lashes.

He dared not.

She was Okmar's.

So was Jehal, himself, if in a different way. He worked for the caravan master, that fat and slovenly son of a lame camel.

Rilah belonged to Okmar. She was a slave.

A slave, though not from the hill-tribes like the others. Her father had been a merchant, a wealthy and well-respected man, before ill fortune struck the family with poverty.

By Inanna, but she was beautiful.

Too good for Okmar.

Too good for Jehal, for that matter.

She should have had a prosperous husband, with a fine house in the city, and two or three plump little babies by now. She should have had slaves of her own, pots of alabaster, necklaces of silver and gold. She should have dined on fowl cooked with dates and honey, instead of the bread and onions and lentils that were the caravan's fare.

An elbow dug into his ribs. "Quit staring or Okmar will pop out your eyes," Andu said.

"I wasn't staring," Jehal said, feeling a flush climb his cheeks.

"Staring like a lamb at the moon." Andu elbowed him again, grinning. "Come help me with the big one before night falls."

They walked past the cook-tent, where other guards and drovers were finishing their meals. The asses, tethered, nosed through bundles of hay. In the purple canopy of dusk, the first stars already sparkled like bright gemstones. Canals and plowed farmlands stretched to either side of the road.

The slaves huddled in a pen made from ropes strung between tall stakes pounded into the earth. Some wore grubby rags and the tattered flaps of sandals. Others wore only dirt, bruises, and whip-weals. They clung together in family groups. A few wept. None spoke. Most were silent. Those that looked at Andu and Jehal did so with dull, hopeless eyes.

Unlike Rilah, these slaves came from the uncivilized hill-tribes who lived on the edges of the kingdoms of Sumer. Raiders captured them to sell to men such as Okmar, who in turn took them to the markets held at the great cities. There was always a demand for such labor.

Jehal pitied them, but knew they would bring a good price. He and Andu nodded to the men who stood watch over the slave-pen and made their way to the big one.

He was easy to find, not only for his size, but because the rest of the slaves avoided him. The caravan had come across him the day before, the large man stumbling along, caked with dust and dried blood, raving in a language none of them could understand. He'd all but collapsed at Okmar's very feet.

No one knew him. No one could guess from what tribe he had come.

And, to Okmar, always practical, it was as good as found money.

"Has he eaten?" Jehal asked.

"Not since yesterday," Andu said. "I gave him water, but he'd take nothing more."

He'd been wounded, as well, when they found him. Scrapes and abrasions covered his body. His face was harrowed by scratches, as if he'd clawed himself with his own fingernails in a frenzy of anguish or grief. Chunks of flesh had been torn from one meaty forearm, leaving raw red marks that looked gouged or gored.

"I wonder what happened to him," Jehal said as they approached the place where the big man lay curled on his side.

Andu shrugged. "Wild dogs?"

They'd washed and bandaged him before putting him among the slaves. He hadn't resisted, didn't seem to know where he was. None of their efforts to speak with him had gained more than meaningless mumbles.

"If he's gone mad, he's gone mad," Okmar had said. "Doesn't matter to us. Look at the size of him, the breadth of his shoulders, the girth of his arms. He's strong as a bull. Someone will pay well for him."

The rest of the slaves continued to give the big one a wide berth, leaving a cleared space around him. Andu had brought a small oil lamp to light their way once they'd left behind the cook-tent's fires. He handed it to Jehal now, who held it aloft.

"He doesn't look well," said Jehal, observing the big man in the lamp's puddling yellow glow.

"It's the fever," said Andu, squatting to unfold a bundle of fresh bandages, salve, and healing herbs. "Infection. I hope we don't have to have his arm off. Okmar won't like that."

"No, he looks worse."

The big one's skin, which had been the fertile color of a riverbank after flood season when they'd found him, had a parched and greyish pallor now, more like badly-mixed clay beginning to dry.

He wasn't moving, either.

"Andu, I think he's dead."

"Okmar will like that even less." Andu poked the big one's shoulder. When there was no response, Andu poked harder, pushing him over onto his back.

The big one's arm flopped out with the peculiar stiff limpness, or limp stiffness, known only to a corpse. His mouth gaped, devoid of breath. A fly alit on his nose.

Andu exhaled a sigh, swore, and called to Maruk. Maruk joined them, looked, and sent his brother Mabot to fetch Okmar.

Okmar came to the slave-pen, annoyed at his evening meal being interrupted. He stood there with mutton grease glistening on his jowls and wine-stains on his chest. Jehal, listening to his conversation with Maruk and Andu, couldn't help but think of pretty Rilah ... no doubt waiting in Okmar's tent.

"Just leave him for now," the caravan master said, belching. "He's not going anywhere. We can see to it in the morning."

Andu frowned, but no one dared to argue. Okmar's irritation made it seem he'd paid good silver for the man, then been cheated by his death, rather than being out no more than the cost of some water and a poultice. He grumbled about it as he stomped off.

They left him.

Jehal unrolled the thin mat of woven reeds he slept upon, and rested his head on the pack in which he kept his belongings. He thought of Rilah again. Would his wages be enough to purchase her freedom? Would Okmar sell it? And what of Rilah, herself? She smiled at him, sometimes. He was younger than Okmar, younger and more handsome. If he was not wealthy, he was hard-working and willing.

His pleasant musings followed him into more pleasant dreams, which made his sudden waking all the more jarring a shock. He bolted upright with screams filling his ears. Startled shouts of alarm sounded from all over the camp.

It took precious scrambling moments before they realized they were not under attack. The commotion was at the slave-pen. Guards came on the run, armed with spears, sticks, whips, and torches. It took precious moments more until they determined the slaves were not attempting an escape, but were instead in a panic.

With Okmar bellowing orders, they forced their way through, subduing the terrified slaves. Several had been injured in the scuffle, knocked down and trampled, bleeding.

At the midst of it –

"You said he was dead!"

"I thought that he was!"

-- was the big one.

Two slaves tried to crawl brokenly away from him, like crippled insects. A third sprawled with his throat torn open, a crimson river's pumping, sluggish, decreasing flow soaking the dry earth under him to mud.

The big one seized a woman by the wrist and hair. He yanked her to him and sank his bloodied teeth into her shoulder. She shrieked. He gnawed. She shrieked again, pulling away. Gristle crackled and bone popped. Her arm twisted off like a joint of roast meat.

And, like a joint of roast meat, the big one hungrily bit and devoured whole dripping chunks.

The woman tottered a few steps, blinking in an expression of astonished surprise, and trailing strings of tendon, then fell over.

"Don't kill him!" yelled Okmar as the guards closed in. "Beat him down, but don't kill him!"

They did as he said, clubbing at the big one with sticks and spear-butts. He fought and thrashed like a madman, biting at them when they pinned his arms and legs. It took five of them to wrestle him to the ground. Andu and Maruk tied him with sturdy rope. Still, he kept thrashing and snapping, making low bestial grunts and groans.

"You fool of a goat's dropping!" Okmar said to Jehal.

"I thought he was dead," Jehal repeated.

"He did look dead," Andu said, in defense of his friend.

Mabot limped over, twin crescents of ragged marks trickling blood down his shin. "Dead men don't take bites from your leg," he said.

Okmar had the guards haul the big one to his knees and began berating him with threats and warnings. It had no more effect now than before. Less, possibly, since the big man no longer even seemed to be trying to understand or communicate. He voiced none of his unfamiliar words, only groaned again, and slobbered his tongue over his lips.

"How is it," Okmar said, shaking his head with disgust, "that, here we are, about to reach the greatest city of Sumer, where a tower tall as the sky is being built to celebrate the founding of a vast empire of all people under one king speaking one civilized tongue ... and this --"

As he said 'this,' he sneered and jabbed his finger in the kneeling slave's face.

Anything else he might have said was lost in an agonized screech.

The crunching teeth did not chop clean through the bone, but broke it with a splintering crack. Fast thinking, and faster action, on the part of the guards let them pry the jaws apart. Okmar stepped back, staring in horror at his mangled, bleeding hand. The finger bent off at an angle like a nearly-broken twig.

Jehal raised his spear, the bronze point gleaming in the torchlight.

"No!" With his other hand, Okmar slapped it aside.

"But --"

"Do you see all this mess?" Okmar demanded, gesturing at the dead, dying, and damaged slaves. "He's cost me real money, now, and I mean to have something back for my pains!"

He had the guards pry the big one's jaws apart again, and use leather cords to hold the mouth wide agape. Then, with a chisel and a stone, they struck out all the teeth.

The big one struggled, but only in an effort to bite again. He seemed oblivious to the pain, though chips and shards fell like pieces of shattered pottery. Even when only hole-riddled gums filled his foaming mouth, he kept snapping uselessly at whatever strayed within reach.

"Clean this up," Okmar went on as Andu bandaged his hand. "Dispose of the dead; tend the rest. Put them out of their misery, if you must. We move on at first light. I want to be to the market early and sell them off, this entire lot of flea-bitten wretches. They're bad luck."

They did as he bade them. Two of the drovers brought their asses and carts to haul away the corpses. One insisted later that the woman whose arm had been torn off hadn't been dead after all, that she'd revived and grabbed at him, tried to kiss him, but his ass bucked and reared and staved in her skull with a hoof. Given the sour stink of barley beer on his breath, nobody lent much credence to his claims.

There was little sleep to be had the rest of that night. Jehal was not the only one who returned to his bed, but tossed and turned in a fitful wakefulness. A mood of unease hung over them all. It kept on as they broke camp and set out.

That the slaves were dispirited was no surprise. They trudged not toward the end of their journey, but toward the start of new lives of hard labor, plowing fields, digging ditches and irrigation canals, mixing straw with mud for the brickmakers, lugging sun-baked bricks for the bricklayers, hauling buckets of water or plaster.

The big one, toothless and muzzled, had to be led on a rope when the whip and goad-pole had no effect.

It all left Okmar in a fouler temper than usual. His head pained him, he said, and his hand throbbed hot with fevered pustules. Rilah tried to appease him with song, to no avail. When Andu offered to look at the wound, Okmar cursed at him. Even Mabot, normally the most genial of men, had harsh words for the cook's boy, accusing him of serving them dung and spoiled food.

Soon, though, they reached the city itself, with its temples and houses, its gardens and gates, its palace. Above the rest rose the tower, the mighty ziggurat, only partially finished, surrounded by wooden scaffolds, ladders, planks, and ropes. Yet, already, it dominated. It challenged the sky.

And the marketplace ...

Oh, the marketplace!

Here were stalls selling sheep skins and leather, flax and linen ... chickens and eggs ... olive oil, fragrant spices ... greens and fruits and figs ... cedarwood ... dried fish and fresh fish ... pottery and baskets ... copper bangles and beads of blue lapis ...

Here were soothsayers, breathing smoke or reading livers. Here were priests of En-Lil and Enki, as well as An and Inanna. Here were married women in veils, and sacred prostitutes with their lips stained berry-red.

Here were musicians, and beggars, and a man walking on his hands, and another juggling torches, and a woman who danced while wearing live snakes.

The caravan passed by on the marketplace's bustling out-skirts, to the slave quarters. The pens held hundreds more, raid-ed from the hill-tribes. Overseers, merchants, craftsmen, and house-masters walked among them, inspecting and haggling. Further on were the pens of cattle, sheep, goats, asses, and camels, where the same activity took place.

Once they had set up and settled in, Okmar surprised them by leaving Maruk in charge and retiring to his lodgings, instead of avidly pursuing his profits. The guards, cooks, and drovers were given a portion of their wages and immediately dispersed to spend it.

"Come drink with me," said Andu, jingling coins. "We'll find other girls you can gaze at yearningly from afar, girls who won't risk you getting your eyes popped out."

Jehal laughed. They went off together into the city and found the Nine Lamps, a loud, lively establishment presided over by a brewstress and her daughters. The wine was good, the beer better. A goat carcass turned, grease sizzling, on a spit above a bed of coals. Layers of opium haze floated in the air, stirred by the trill of reed flutes.

Time passed pleasantly.

Until a man burst in through the curtain of strung sections of dried river reed stalks, making them clatter. Blood ran from many wounds. His arms clutched his sundered midsection, hands filled with a slippery mass of entrails.

Those nearest him recoiled, some with cries of their own. The man blundered a few steps further. His eyes rolled like those of an ox at slaughter. "They're coming!" he cried, then vomited up a glut of bile.

Women screamed and men shouted. The wounded man swayed in place, gurgled, and pitched headlong to the straw-covered dirt floor. A stain spread beneath him.

More screams and shouts came from outside of the Nine Lamps. Inside, after a moment of shock, dozens of alarmed voices arose at once – was the city under attack? Enemies of

Sumer? Soldiers of a rival king? People sprang to their feet. Beer spilled. Opium pipes tipped, spilling smoldering embers into the straw.

Andu, kneeling by the man sprawled in his own guts, looked up at Jehal. "He's dead --"

The man groaned. He pushed himself up with his arms. Intestines swung, dangling and dripping, out of his opened belly.

"Andu!" Jehal jumped over an upended bench, grabbed his startled friend by the shoulder, and yanked him backward just as the man lunged.

The dead man. For so he was, and so he had to be. No one could be so eviscerated and still live.

Jehal and Andu crashed into a table, knocking it over, spilling more bowls of beer. The dead man seized another victim, instead, a wizened old man frowning at the disturbances from a bewildered opium stupor. His teeth ripped into the old man's bald scalp, peeling away a leathery flap.

"What's going on?" Andu asked. "Jehal, what's happening here?"

"I ..." Jehal shook his head, which still swam with drunkenness.

Confusion and terror inflamed the patrons of the Nine Lamps. Even as they tried to rush outside, other figures tried to shove their way in ... lurching, mauled figures, with limbs missing, with faces half torn off.

"We have to get out of here!" Jehal pulled Andu up from the floor.

"They're ... they're corpses ... look at them, Jehal, they're corpses but they move, they walk ..."

With the entrance blocked by the murderous dead and their prey, Jehal cast his gaze wildly about. He saw the brewstress waving people toward a short flight of mudbrick steps. He and Andu rushed that way and emerged onto a flat rooftop courtyard with a rail fence, where woven grass shades held aloft on poles provided some relief from the heat of the day.

It also provided a view of the violent carnage in the streets. The city gates thronged with frantic crowds trying to escape. The marketplace had become a killing ground.

Again and again, they saw it ... someone would fall, savaged and dying ... then rise up, heedless of his or her wounds ... consumed by a ravenous hunger for the flesh of the living ...

Other survivors had likewise taken refuge on rooftops, defending the narrow stairs, or climbing up ladders and walls. They called back and forth, one group to another, hoping for answers or plans or advice.

Evil spirits, most agreed. A curse, a spell, angry gods.

A disease, claimed a few. A plague, a sickness and contagion.

No one was safe. The dead turned on their own friends, their own family. Pleading was useless. Their own names brought no recognition, falling as if on deaf ears or dull wits or dead minds. They cared for nothing but their hunger.

Those who fought back found that even spears and sickle-swords seemed to do little good. The risen felt no pain. Cut their legs out from under them and they'd crawl, or drag themselves along. They were slow-moving and clumsy, but they kept on, relentless.

It started in the slave-market, some said. Started there and spread, and those who weren't killed outright, those who came away bitten or scratched, those still succumbed to it, as if stricken by poison.

At that, Jehal and Andu exchanged a suddenly-sobered glance.

"The big one," said Andu. "You were right. He was dead. All the ones that he injured ... he bit Mabot, and Okmar, too --"

"Rilah!" Jehal ran to the edge of the roof and swung a leg over the fence.

Andu ran after him. "What are you doing? You can't think to go find her!"

"I'm going."

"She's a slave --"

"I don't care."

"Jehal, she must already be --"

"I have to know!"

"You'll only get yourself killed. Don't do it. Don't be a fool."

"I'll come back."

Jehal jumped into the street. Sun-baked blood dried on mudbrick, like potter's glaze on clay. The nearest group of the shambling dead turned toward him. He hesitated, knees weak and bowels watery. They were much closer from down here than they'd been from the roof.

Andu yelled at him from above. Jehal snapped to his senses and began running.

Here was a wailing woman cradling the body of her child, which then stirred in her arms. Her wails turned to joyful weeping ... she leaned to kiss the little face ... then shrieked as the child's teeth sank into her lip.

Here was a soothsayer, who must not have foreseen these omens; the sheep's liver she'd been reading was cast aside as she buried her head into a man's belly in search of something more tasty.

And here was a wealthy man's corpse, still gleaming with jewelry his killers had ignored. A beggar crept from hiding to strip him of his gold, only to have the corpse sit up and chew through his throat.

If the marketplace had become a killing ground, the slave quarters were worse. Clouds of flies, buzzing green-black, roiled over body parts, offal, and unrecognizable lumps of meat. Some of the dead had not been able to escape their pens and milled there, groaning.

Jehal almost laughed when he saw the big one among them. The big one, toothless and muzzled, who'd brought this horror down on their heads ... when had it been too late? If they hadn't found him, if Okmar hadn't put him in with the slaves ...

Not that it mattered, not now.

He almost laughed, yes, but it would have been a mad, mirthless laugh, bitter as the dregs of old, cold tea.

A guard's spear, the bronze point bloodied, sticky hand-prints along the haft, had been discarded or dropped between the pens. Jehal picked it up. It failed to make him feel much safer. He did not want to speculate on whose it might have been, or what must have become of its owner.

Okmar's tent, over where the caravan masters took their lodgings, was silent. Whether it was the silence of abandonment, of the undisturbed, or of the dead, Jehal didn't know. He approached quietly, cautiously, tense with apprehension.

He used the spear to lift aside the tent flap and peered in.

The tent's furnishings were strewn about in disarray, as if a struggle had taken place. Jehal's heart sank. A curve of splintered wood and a tangle of strings – part of a broken lyre – lay near a man's fat-ankled and grimy foot.

There was Okmar, face down, with his limbs splayed, not moving. A few flies circled above him. His skin looked mottled, both greyish and dark, like the rind of a bad fruit. On the side of his head was a split gash, clotted with hair and blood. Another curve of splintered wood – the other part of a broken lyre – jutted from his eye socket.

"Rilah ..." Jehal said.

He heard a gasp and a rustle, swiftly muffled.

"Rilah?" he said again, louder, hardly daring to hope.

A sheepskin by the bed moved, drawing back to reveal Rilah's frightened, tearful face.

"You --" His breath caught. "You're alive."

She slowly stood up, letting the sheepskin drop. Her shoulders slumped in despair. Stains spotted the front of her simple robe.

"I wish it wasn't you," she said, voice quavering. "Please, be quick."

"What?"

"I killed him," she said. "I'm to be put to death, I killed him, I'm only a slave and --"

"Are you hurt? Did he ... did he attack you?"

"He tried to ... how did you know?"

"Did he bite you?" Jehal repeated. "Scratch you?"

"No ... just ..." She showed him her arms, bruised with fingermarks, but not scratched.

"Tell me what happened."

Okmar, Rilah said, hadn't felt any better after retiring to his tent. His hand pained him, and his head. He felt sick, feverish and nauseous, unable to rest. He didn't want food, water, music, or anything. Finally, he'd fallen asleep.

"It ... it was a strange sleep," she went on. "He didn't snore. He's always snored. Then I wondered if it *was* sleep, if I should do something, fetch someone. But he'd forbidden me to, so I obeyed. I fell asleep, myself. I woke to hear him getting up. And the ... the way he looked ... the way he seized and pulled me ... the way he opened his mouth ..."

In her terror, without thinking, Rilah had struck Okmar with the lyre. It broke against the side of his head. When he went for her again, she'd jabbed it at him. Only meaning to ward him off, she said, but the end had plunged into his eye.

"He fell." She glanced at Okmar, and glanced away, shuddering. "Dead. I'd killed him."

"And he stayed that way?" Jehal asked. He prodded Okmar's leg with the spear, but the caravan master did not move. Even when he punctured the skin, wincing as he did so, Okmar did not move. Nor did he bleed, except for an oozing dribble.

Rilah stared at Jehal. "Stayed that way?" she echoed.

"Don't you know what's going on out there?"

"I ... I hid," she said. "I didn't know what else to do. There was such noise ... yelling and ... horrible noises. I thought they'd found out. I thought someone would come for me. They will. They'll put me to death --"

"No," Jehal said. He drew her close, resting his chin atop her head. "No, I won't let them, I won't let anyone harm you."

She clung to him, shaking and sobbing. Although he'd imagined her in his arms many times, it had never quite been like this.

A low, hungry groaning made them whirl. It was not Okmar; Okmar remained motionless, cooling and flyblown. The groaning came from outside, followed by shadows falling across the tent.

"Come on."

"What is that?"

"The dead."

"What?"

Holding her hand, he led her behind him, with the spear preceding them both. They rushed out of the tent. Rilah stifled a scream when she saw the corpses stumbling toward them.

"Maruk," Jehal said. "Mabot. Ah, no."

It made sense, of course ... Mabot had been bitten, and Maruk would have taken faithful care of his brother once the fever set in ... but when Mabot died and rose again, he would not have been bound by similar brotherly loyalty.

More closed in – other guards, drovers, slaves, cooks. The ones still trapped in the pens strained against the fences, clawing at the air, gnashing their teeth.

Dead or not, Maruk and Mabot had been his friends. Jehal didn't want to fight them. The brothers, however, had no such sentiments. They came at him with arms outstretched and jaws gaping.

"Jehal!" Rilah cried.

He stuck the bronze spearhead into Mabot's chest. The metal grated on rib, and punched through muscle and gristle to pierce the heart. But Mabot kept coming. Jehal yanked the spear back. Sludge, like runny mashed figs spilled out.

"How did you kill Okmar?"

"I told you! I hit him with my lyre, then --"

Jehal thrust the spear at Mabot's eye, but the dead man stumbled over a gnawed-looking severed leg. His head twisted. The bronze point sank into his temple, instead. Mabot twitched, then dropped, his impaled head tugging the spear, and Jehal's arm, down with him.

He lost his grip. Maruk's hands, not warm but not cold, clumsy but still large and strong, caught at him and grappled. They fell, Jehal on the bottom, Maruk's heavy but hideously writhing deadweight atop him. The impact coughed tepid carrion breath from his lungs into Jehal's face. Jehal gagged.

Somehow, he wedged his forearm under Maruk's chin as the teeth clashed, barely missing the tip of his nose. They struggled in the mud.

Rilah shrieked. The spear shaft cracked down on Maruk's skull and snapped in half. The butt end clattered off Jehal's forehead. He groped for it, got it, and rammed it upward with all his strength. The jagged length of wood skewered through the roof of Maruk's mouth.

A thick, reeking slime gushed down the spear-shaft. Jehal let go, rolling and twisting out from under Maruk.

Both brothers were unmoving corpses now. But the rest kept coming, groaning their hunger.

Jehal seized Rilah's hand again.

They ran.

The dead were everywhere.

In the slave quarters and the marketplace. Crowded at the gates. Filling the streets.

They made it to the Nine Lamps and found it overrun.

The rooftops were awash in blood.

"Jehal!"

He looked up. And up.

Until he saw Andu waving from high above.

Andu, and others who'd scaled the unfinished ziggurat's scaffolding and rickety ladders, which the dead could not climb.

Jehal and Rilah joined them.

From there, they watched.

The dead swarmed like locusts.

The living scattered in all directions, never looking back. With them went all hope of a single empire under one king and one rule and one language.

The dead held the great city then, in the lands between the rivers, lands rich with silt and clay. They held it, all but the unfinished zigguraut, far from five thousand cubits high.

All but the jewel of Babylonia, a tower to the sky.

GOOD BOY

Defeat. Submission. Surrender.

No anger. No fight, no defiance.

She does not growl. She does not raise her hackles or bare her teeth.

Resignation. Acceptance.

She gives throat. She gives underbelly. She cowers.

All without moving. All in her posture. All in her expression, demeanor, and manner. All in her scent, in the shaking sigh of her breath.

Least of the pack. Lowest of status.

Sit. Stay.

She sits. She stays.

Can't hunt. Can't fight. Can't run.

The Mate ...

Coward. Slinking yellow-smell coward, shifting eyes, guilt.

And the Bitch. Strong. Dominant. Smug.

They will leave her. Abandon her. A burden. Without use, without value.

"You know we have to. We can't take her with us. It's impossible. She'll only slow us down, get us all killed."

"But we can't just --"

"She can't walk!"

"She can ..."

"Barely. For how long? How far? Are you going to carry her?"

"Damn it, Angie! Listen to yourself! She's my girlfriend!"

"So you'll stay here and die with her?"

"Maybe it isn't as bad out there as --"

"Don't be an ass, Ron! You saw the news. We all did."

"Someone will come. The National Guard, someone."

"Maybe they will, maybe they won't. For now, all I know is that we're on our own. You know that, too. If we want to live through this, we've got to move."

"Live through it, yeah, but what about living with ourselves?"

"Oh for fuck's sake! Spare me the morality lesson. Next you'll be telling me again how it was all your fault, so you owe her, you're obligated."

"It was. I do."

"It was an accident. She's been using it to chain you down ever since. You were going to break up with her anyway --"

"Shh! She'll hear you!"

"So what? In case you didn't notice, we've got serious problems. Either weapon up and come with us, or stay here taking care of your crippled girlfriend until those things overrun this place."

The sirens. Rising and falling, ceaseless ululation. Urge to howl in sympathy, in concert, in answer.

Sirens, shots, screams.

Her hand rests, trembling, upon Baxter's head. Between his ears, fuzzy triangles perked upright, listening. Her fingers stroke his fur. Black with brown. Shepherd-mix, they call him.

Urge to howl, urge to growl, urge to bark.

No.

Training and discipline.

On-duty.

Working.

Dedicated.

Good Boy.

Baxter sits beside her Chair. Alert. His harness on, straps buckled, handle with its rubber grip ready. Vest. Collar. Leash.

She speaks. "Ron?"

The others turn to her. The Mate furtive. Shame-faced. Hangdog. Guilty. The Bitch irritated. Sneering. Impatient.

"Go," she says. "Just ... go."

"Julia ..."

"See? You heard her. She knows. Come on." The Bitch, grasping the Mate's arm. Claiming. Possessive. Vindicated.

The Mate pulls away from the Bitch. Approaches. Kneels. Looks stricken, but that *smell*, that coward-yellow smell, is stronger.

"This isn't right," he says. "If we got a van or something --"

"Take a look out the window," says the Bitch. "The roads are a crazy nightmare. We'll be lucky to make it on foot."

More screams, more shots. A dead-moaning, low, but louder. Gaining. Growing.

"I can't just leave you like this." The Mate, touching the Chair, touching a wheel, looking from it to the metal crutch-sticks where they lean. "If we --"

"No, Ron," Julia says. Like her posture, her voice is defeat, is surrender, is resignation and loss and hurt. "You have to leave. You have to go, now, while there's a chance."

"What about you?"

"I'll be fine. I've got Baxter. He'll take care of me. He's my Good Boy."

The tail, wag-thump. Despite urge to growl, howl, bark. Despite urge to snarl.

"We'll find help. As soon as we're somewhere safe, somewhere defensible --"

"Yeah. Okay."

"Hurry up, Ron," the Bitch says. Strong legs. Straight spine. Whole. Healthy. Pack on her back. Gun at her hip. Looks and smells alive. Eager. Triumphant.

"We will," the Mate – the Abandoner – goes on. "We'll come back for you. I'll come back for you. I promise."

"Sure." Her hand, on Baxter's head, trembles more, and she buries her fingers in his thick scruff-fur.

Silver-white poison smile from the Bitch. "Sure," she echoes.

The Abandoner stands. His throat hitches. He gulps. "Jules, I'm so sorry ... about this, about ... everything ..."

Wanting permission, forgiveness, absolution. Wanting comfort. Wanting reassurance.

Urge to snarl.

Coward. Wretched, weak, yellow-slink coward.

"You'd better go." Julia turns her face away. Shuts her eyes. Lips pressed together. Submission, surrender, but moment of dignity. Moment of head-held-high.

Voices. Hallway. Neighbors and friends. Not all. Some hadn't come home since it started. There'd been arguments – it was an internet hoax, it was the end times, it was a movie promo, it was aliens/terrorists/God. Some left. Some stayed. Grouped together, or locked in alone. Furniture, wood, and junk tumbled into the stairwells. Televisions, radios. Waiting for it to get better. Or worse.

Calling. "Angie! Ron! What's the hold-up? Are we bugging out of here, or what?"

"On our way!" replies the Bitch. She hefts a ball-bat.

The Mate/Abandoner hesitates. Starts to lean over, as if for a kiss. Withdraws. "I can't. What if they get here first? What if they find you, and ... and ..."

More dead-moans. Close. Very close. Screams.

"Holy shit! It's Mr. Parkins!"

A shriek. A shot.

"Did he bite you?"

"No, no, thank you, Jesus, thank you!"

"Dude, you blew the landlord's head off!"

"But he was okay, he was okay this morning!"

"He fucking wasn't okay anymore!"

"Where's his wife?"

"Hell if I know!"

"Move it! We gotta go, we gotta go *now*! Haul some ass!"

The Bitch grasps the Mate/Abandoner's arm again. "Come on!"

"I ... I can't ..."

"There's nothing else you can do for her now!"

"She's right," Julia says.

"Unless," the Bitch adds, with another poison smile, "you want to put her out of her misery before they *do* get to her."

"Jesus, Angie!"

He looks shocked. Looks disgusted, looks appalled.

But he considers it.

Julia knows that he does. She flinches. She clutches Baxter's collar.

Urge to snarl and this time *yes*, this time *snarl*, hackles raised and teeth bared. No longer sitting. Ears forward. Eyes narrowed. Snarl and *growl*.

"Go!" Julia cries. "Just *go* already!"

They go.

The door closes. Their steps sound in the hall, diminishing, moving away. Voices mutter, indistinct. Outside are car-horns, car-alarms, the dead-moaning, a rattle of shots, an explosion. Another dog barks, far away, blocks away, confused. Glass breaks. A man laughs, mindless mad-laugh, cackling.

Julia sobs. She slumps in the Chair, covering her face. The tears drip through her fingers. Baxter goes up on his hindlegs, hooks his forepaws over the armrest, pushes his muzzle at her, licks her chin. Nuzzles and chuffs. She hugs him. The tears wet his fur.

"Oh, Baxter. Oh, Baxter, what are we going to do?"

Finally, the sobbing stops. He trots to the table, fetches the tissue box, brings it to her. She wipes her cheeks, her eyes. She blows her nose.

"Good boy," she says. "Crutches? Baxter, bring me my crutches?"

He does so, fetching them one at a time, carrying them by the leather pads fitted around their middles. Julia puts her arms through the cuffs, braces the rubber-tipped ends, and heaves herself upright. Baxter stays poised and alert at her side, watching her, as she maneuvers on her thin and twisted legs. She turns the door-lock and hooks the chain.

They go to the window. They look out.

Smoke billows and blows. Cars are on the sidewalks, on the lawns, upside-down in the streets. Bodies sprawl. People run. The dead moan and stumble. There is blood, so much blood, blood in smears and streaks, blood in widening puddles, blood in splatters.

Two children crouch atop a truck that has fallen sideways; the dead crowd around it, their dead arms reaching, their dead hands seeking. A man tries to clamber over a fence, they catch his feet, they drag him down, his scream is short. A boy on a bike weaves through the throngs. He has a gun. A dead man lurches toward him. The boy fires. The dead man's head splits apart. Slimy chunks spray across a stop sign. His body blunders another two paces before collapsing in a motionless heap.

Tires screech as a car skids around a corner, bumps up onto the curb, plows into a brick wall. The hood crumples. The horn blares. A dazed woman staggers out. She calls for help. She moves toward a man in a police uniform. He turns. Half his face is gone in a raw, ragged flap of meat. He falls upon her, and what's left of his mouth chews into her throat.

Teenagers in boots and black leather, with wild hair and metal studs through their lips and eyebrows, charge in a hunt-pack. They whoop war-shouts as they swing crowbars, fire-hatchets, shovels. They leap over corpses. They smash skulls. The ones they hit drop and do not move again. Then a bald, wiry, naked man with one arm ending in a mangled stump bursts from an alleyway. The teenager he springs at thrusts out a defensive hand, catching the bald man by the chin, but two fingers poke between the rows of teeth. The bald man chomps down. The teenager squeals, yanking back a bleeding ruin.

Another teen, matted magenta dreadlocks flying, rushes up and buries an ax-blade in the back of the bald scalp. Then, with barely a moment's acknowledging gaze, let alone a word of apology, decapitates the one with the bitten hand. Metal studs glint as the severed head bounces into the gutter.

A big, bearded man hurls a trash can through a storefront. More glass shatters. An alarm warbles. He starts grabbing items, stuffing them into a pillowcase. He doesn't notice the grey and broken form of an elderly woman crawling on her elbows, not until she sinks her teeth into his hamstring.

Julia yanks down the blinds. The room goes dim and shadowed. She totters gracelessly to the Chair and drops into it, sobbing again. Baxter ignores his training and huddles halfway on her lap. She hugs him and pets him.

Good Boy.

They wait.

He needs to go Outside, but he can hold it.

No one comes back. Not the Mate, Ron, who is only the Abandoner now. Not the Bitch. Not anyone.

The shots and screams heard through the window gradually taper off. The dead-moans increase. They see a man jump from a ledge, watch him plummet, watch him land in a crumpled and blood-leaking heap ... and see him stir, see him struggle to his feet ... see him move in a listless, hitching gait to join the other wandering corpses.

Baxter knows his duty. He brings the case with Julia's medicines. He brings her bottles of water, soda, and juice, gripping them gingerly in his jaws. Then the fridge-box for keeping the drinks cold is less cold. The lights are off. The television stays dark. The oven-box and microwave-box for cooking her food do not work.

"The power's out," she says. "That means no elevator, either. We're stuck here, unless we take the stairs, and ..." She hits her own leg with a curled fist. Self-hate, self-anger in her look and in her smell.

The need to go Outside is becoming urgent, but when he stands by the door, Julia shakes her head. "We can't, I'm sorry, not now, we just can't."

She has other food and eats that. Food from the fridge-box and freezer-box as it warms, before it spoils. She fills Baxter's food and water dispensers to the top. She fills other bowls and jugs with water.

"In case we lose that, too," she says.

Soon he needs to go Outside worse than ever. He might have to use the floor, piddle like a puppy. Humiliating. Not Good Boy, but Bad Dog. He whines and prances. She puts down papers. Piddle-papers, for a puppy. Hot stream gush and trickle, and shame, but he goes. Then he skulks behind the couch with head low, with tail tucked under. He cringes from the scolding that is sure to come ... but does not.

"It's all right," she tells him. "It's okay, you had to go."

And she, though she doesn't go Outside, doesn't make the whoosh-watering flush in the bathroom, either. Not after the first time, when the sound seems huge in the dead-moaning stillness. Not when it's followed by a thud overhead, and heavy thumps and dragging from somewhere upstairs.

They eat, they sleep, they wait. Baxter guards the door. Without the heater-vents blowing, it is cold. He fetches Julia's slippers, a blanket.

Another day passes. And another.

Still, no one comes back.

"They must not have made it," Julia whispers. "Ron, and Angie, and them. Or they did find someplace safe, but couldn't risk returning. If they even would have. Ron, maybe ... if Angie let him ... that bitch ..."

Sour smells begin to seep from the fridge-box and freezer-box. Rancid and spoiling. They leave it shut. Julia eats food from the cupboards and cans.

"We're on our own, aren't we?" she asks. "Even if anybody else survived, they won't know we're here."

Baxter pushes his nose under her hand until she strokes his head. He thumps his tail dolefully, dutifully. He gazes up at her with the big sad eyes.

"Do you think they're all dead? They can't *all* be, can they? Not the whole world."

They sleep. The rooms are becoming stinky, stinky from the spoiled-smells in the kitchen, stinky from the piddle-papers and the bathroom because they both still have to go. Julia could use a B-A-T-H, and Baxter almost starts to wish for one himself.

But Outside is no better. When Julia inches open a window, the rot-smell floods in, mixed with smoke smells and burn smells. There are fires, buildings on fire but no firetrucks with wailing sirens to make Baxter want to howl.

"Maybe it's wrong of me, selfish, to keep you here," she says. "Maybe you'd do fine out there on your own. I haven't seen any ... you know, animals ... affected. And the ... people ... don't even seem to notice them. They only want to ... go after ... other people."

It's true; there are animals everywhere. Rats, gulls, crows, and pigeons have a feast. So do the possums, and the raccoons. They see cats, countless cats, darting into and out of myriad hiding places, flattening their ears and hissing at the dead.

Once, a horse goes by, dried blood crusted onto its empty saddle, reins trailing, ignored by the shuffling corpses as its hooves clop hollowly on the pavement. Another time, of all things, a pot-bellied pig waddles, snuffling down the street.

And dogs, yes. Dogs, singly or in pairs or packs ... Baxter's ears prick up whenever he hears them barking, squabbling over whatever they've been able to forage and scavenge and scrounge. He doesn't bark in reply. But he yearns to.

"What will we do when our food runs out? Our water? Even if we could find some stuff in the other apartments, how much? For how long? Then there's my medication ... I was almost due for a refill ... down to my last few pain pills before hitting the reserve stash ... what then?"

She decides they should look around while it's quiet. In a kitchen drawer is a tenderizer mallet, sturdy handle, blocky metal head. Julia sets this in her lap. She adds a big knife and a flashlight. She unlocks the door and looks out. Baxter is beside her, ears up, muscles tense, nose sniffing.

Nothing moves. The rot and blood stink is thick. Mr. Perkins lies splayed on the rug. Old and fat. Greasy-grey. A bite-sized chunk gone from his arm. Most of his head gone from his body, pasted in lumps to the wall.

Julia wheels the Chair into the hallway. She cannot get it past Mr. Perkins, and Baxter takes the man's pajama sleeve in his teeth. He pulls and drags until the Chair can go by.

"Good Boy," Julia whispers. A faint giggle comes from her; it sounds not-right. Then she almost cries. The Chair leaves tracks in the slime that came from Mr. Perkins.

Some doors are shut. Some are open. A cat, Little-Tina-from-201's cat, Princess, fluffy and squash-faced, hisses at them with tail puffed, and runs downstairs.

In the open apartments, clothes and things have been scattered, half-packed, left behind. Pictures are down from the walls, gone from the tables. There are more fridge-boxes of spoiled food. They find a few cans and packages, which Julia puts in the Chair's shopping-basket. They find a goldfish bowl, where the goldfish floats upside-down at the top.

From the end of the hall comes a slow creaking sound. The door to Mr. and Mrs. Perkins' apartment stands ajar. The sound is behind it. Julia pushes it with the tenderizer mallet. Inside, hanging from the ceiling fan with a rope around her neck, Mrs. Perkins sways and turns, back and forth. Her dangling legs below her nightgown are dark, bloated. One of her slippers has fallen off. The bare foot is swollen, almost black.

Julia makes a half-gasp, half-shriek, noise and puts her hand over her mouth.

Back and forth goes Mrs. Perkins. Swaying. Turning. Slowly revolving. Curlers in her hair. Dried urine on the floor. Dried blood on her chin, splashed down her front.

Mrs. Perkins lifts her head. It lolls, crooked, against one shoulder. The rope digs into her throat. Her eyes stare, milky, clouded. She tries to dead-moan and only gurgles. Her fingers, bunched like bent sticks, reach for Julia. She chews hungrily at the air.

Baxter growls. He puts himself in front of the Chair. Once, there were cookies baked here, and a tin by the clock held doggie treats. Maybe the tin still does hold doggie treats, but he does not want them. Julia sobs. She rolls the Chair backward, into the hall again. Baxter follows. She closes the door.

A clumsy thudding of footsteps. A shape staggers out of the stairwell ... a boy ... Matthew-from-upstairs ... who would sometimes throw a ball for Baxter in the park.

Not anymore. Matthew dead-moans. His hair sticks up. His jeans are torn. He rushes at Julia as fast as he can. She screams. Baxter leaps, barking. Matthew does not stop. Baxter snaps at him, Bad Dog to snap at a boy, but snaps anyway. Matthew still does not stop. Baxter jumps on Matthew, knocks him down, holds him pinned there with forepaws on Matthew's shoulders, snarling into Matthew's face. Matthew struggles.

"Baxter, move!" shouts Julia.

He springs aside. She rolls. The Chair's wheel runs into Matthew's ribs. Matthew gnashes his teeth – he is missing one, a gap in the white row – at her feet where they ride propped on the footrests.

Julia raises the tenderizer mallet high in both hands. She brings it down hard. She spills out of the Chair as she does so. The mallet's heavy metal-block head crunches into Matthew's forehead, breaking his skull, driving bone-edges into the cold wet brain-mush.

The Chair squirts backward down the hall, shooting out from under Julia as she falls. She lands partway on Matthew, who has gone limp. Uttering terrible gagging groans of revulsion, she pushes herself off the boy. She collapses, crying, on the rug.

Baxter goes to her. With nudges and nuzzles, he coaxes her to get up, to haul herself into the Chair with her arms, while bracing her thin and twisted legs. They return to their own apartment. Julia curls on the bed and hugs Baxter. He rests his chin on her chest until she sleeps.

She does not want to leave again.

Soon, the water is almost gone. Soon, the food is almost gone.

Soon, Julia just sits in the Chair by the window. She holds the last pill-bottle, her reserve stash, and a can of warm soda. Baxter cocks his head, perturbed, when he sees her pour all the pills into her palm. She takes them, swallows them with a gulp of the soda. She drops the empty pill-bottle.

"Baxter ... who's a Good Boy, who's my Good Boy?"

He wags his tail, though his head remains cocked.

"Do you want to go Outside?"

An eager whine escapes him, despite his uneasy feeling.

"You'll have to go by yourself," she says, rolling the Chair to the door. "But you're my Good Boy, such a Good Boy, so smart and brave ... I know you'll be okay."

She unlocks the door, takes off the chain, opens it. The hallway is quiet beyond. Not even Princess the cat is around.

"I love you, Baxter." Her voice slurs, as if suddenly drowsy. "I hate to leave you like this, I'm so sorry, I love you, you took care of me so well."

With a sigh, she slumps in the Chair, her cheek on her shoulder. She mumbles. She smiles. Then she is still.

Outside. She opened the door for him, she asked if he wanted to go Outside, which he does. But he doesn't. Something is wrong. The way she sleeps isn't sleep. He remembers his training, his duty.

The phone, knock the phone from its cradle, step on the big button with his paw. It does not click. Does not buzz.

He trots to the door and barks. Sharp, loud barks. Come-help-me barks.

No one comes.

He trots back to Julia and works his muzzle under her hand, which lies cool and slack on her thigh. She does not pet him, does not stroke his fur, does not scratch the top of his head between his ears.

Baxter rests his chin in her lap, whining softly.

Then he trots to the door again, and ventures into the hall. He picks his way down the stairs, through the jumble of junk and furniture that had been dumped there as a barricade. He squeezes through a gap. Finally, he is Outside.

The air stinks of the dead, moaning as they shuffle aimlessly along the sidewalks and streets. They ignore Baxter. They are oblivious to him.

He lifts his nose, sniffing carefully for other traces of scent. He smells other animals, other dogs, even the horse with the empty saddle. He smells people, distant but living. Warm and sweaty people.

Some of the scents are familiar. He follows those, tracking them. Friends and neighbors. Ron. Maybe Angie. He'll find them. Find them, bring them back, bring them home.

Because Julia will be hungry, and he is a Good Boy.

THOUGHT HE
WAS A GONER

"Go on." Mary Norris gave Sarah a nudge. "Go talk to him."

Sarah took a half-step, then hesitated. "Do you really think I ought to?"

"Well, *I* wouldn't." Rolling her eyes, Mary affected the worldly manner of their teacher, Miss Phelps. "But, since *you* fancy him, you might as well."

"*Mary* fancies Tommy Lowgate," Cecily confided to Peg and Meg, without glancing up from the hopscotch she'd almost finished drawing.

"I do not!" cried Mary, blushing the bright hue of a hothouse rose.

It might have been becoming on another girl. On sunny-blonde Cecily, perhaps. Or Sarah herself, whose curls were as black and shiny and glossy as fresh ink. On carrot-topped Mary, with her freckly cheese-curd complexion, the effect was fevered and blotchy.

Peg and Meg, twins, cupped their hands over their mouths and tittered. Mary blushed brighter than ever. She threw a quick look in the direction of the other girls, but the older ones were chatting beside the lunch-room with the older boys, and the younger ones from Mrs. Daunley's class had a jumping-rope and sang that new song about the man with the cat he couldn't get rid of, no matter how hard he tried.

"... but the cat came back ... the very next day ..."

Sarah, twirling a ringlet, gazed over at the boy who sat reading in the shade of the big spreading oak.

"... yes, the cat came back ..."

The new boy.

Herbie West.

Beyond him, on a grassy sward, his classmates ran and shouted and kicked a ball back and forth. The smaller boys, armed with sticks, played war.

"... they thought he was a goner ..."

At lunch, Herbie West never threw crusts or spat cherry pips. During study-hour, he didn't draw rude sketches, pull girls' pigtails, make faces, or whisper when the headmaster stepped into the hall for a nip of what he called 'the revivifying' from the flask he kept in his coat.

"... but the cat came back ..."

No, Herbie West sat just as he sat now, by himself. Sat by himself and read.

"... he just wouldn't stay away!"

Quiet. Polite and soft-spoken, as Sarah's mother would have said.

And smart, too. Sarah had overheard Mr. Pym telling Miss Phelps that the West boy was "sharp as a tack, smart as a whip, cleverest student I've ever had ... but insolent ... you wouldn't know it to look at him, meek as he is, but twice now he's corrected *me* in front of the entire class."

Sarah thought this was especially brave. Much braver and much cleverer than most boys, whose idea of wit was to make fake flatulence-noises and blame them on each other.

"But she's right," Cecily said. "Recess won't last much longer. Go talk to him. Don't be a ninny."

"Do I look nice?" Sarah asked.

"Yes," grumbled Mary.

The twins vigorously agreed.

She considered skipping, but decided against it and went at an idle-seeming stroll, instead, as if she were simply going for a walk around the schoolyard that happened to bring her course near the big spreading oak.

As she approached, she let herself steal several peeks at him, though always ready to quickly pretend *not* to be, just in case he noticed.

Herbie West wasn't a tall boy. He was thin, and quite pale, with fine hair the color of buttermilk. His eyes, behind spectacles, were a very light blue. They remained fixed intently on his book, a great heavy thick thing, unlike their school readers and primers. Sarah saw that the pages were covered with dense printing, big words in small letters, blocks of it broken only by diagrams and illustrations.

Feeling suddenly both giddy and shy, she stopped just within the patch of cool shade. She twisted her toe against the grass, turning her ankle this way and that.

"Hello, Herbie," she said.

He twitched as if she'd startled him, and shut the book with a musty kind of thump. His light blue eyes were wide through the lenses.

"Hello," she said again, smiling.

"I prefer to be addressed as Herbert," he said. He had such a soft voice, she had to lean forward to hear. "Or West, if you rather."

"Oh ... sorry ... Herbert." She bolstered her smile, which tried to falter, and resumed twirling the long black ringlet that dangled beside her cheek. "I'm Sarah. Sarah Grantham."

Herbert West nodded. There followed a slight, awkward pause.

"What are you reading?" Sarah asked brightly.

"Nothing of interest to you." He placed a hand on the cover. "A medical book."

"Medical? You mean, doctoring?"

"Sort of."

"Sort of? How so?"

"It's to do with ..." Herbert took a breath. "It's to do with anatomy and dissections."

"With what and what?" She frowned, but made sure it was her pretty frown, not the sulky one her mother said made her look like a bulldog deprived its bone.

"Anatomy is the study of human physiology. Dissection is the more practical method of determining form and function through surgical exploration --"

Sarah tilted her head. "Cutting up dead people?"

He winced ever-so-slightly, one eye narrowing and the corner of his mouth on that side tucking into a tight line. "Dissecting cadavers."

"Have you done that?"

"No." The wince deepened into a brief scowl, then smoothed. "But I will, one day. I'm going to attend the medical school at Miskatonic University. Soon. Headmaster Abelton says I'll be an excellent candidate for early admission."

Most of that made scant sense to Sarah, but she didn't let on. She skipped up next to him and sat down, smoothing her skirt over her knees. "My grandfather died last winter," she said.

This, she reasoned, would give them something in common – rumor had it that his parents had both recently died, which was why he'd been sent here to live with his two maiden aunties.

Herbert West, however, did not seem inclined to commiserate over shared losses. "Did you see him?"

"No! He died in the hospital."

"I meant, after that. For a funeral."

"Oh," said Sarah. "Oh, yes. We had him laid out in the parlor for a few days, so that everyone could pay their respects while waiting for my uncle and his family to come from Chicago."

"So, you did see him. What was it like?"

She tilted her head the other way. "Not like he was sleeping. That's what they all said, how peaceful he looked, like he was sleeping, but I didn't think so."

"What did you think?"

"He looked ... dead," she said. "He was all grey, his lips blue. Sunken-looking. Stiff and cold. His skin felt --" She caught herself with a guilty squirm.

But Herbert hadn't missed her slip. "You touched him?"

"My cousins and I, we dared each other," Sarah admitted. "I touched his hand. Where it was, you know, folded like this on his chest."

His nod this time was encouraging. "How did it feel?"

"Stiff and cold, like I said, but also ... I don't really know."

"Waxy? Like a candle, or a cake of soap?"

"Yes! Yes, just like that! Not quite greasy, but somehow kind of ..."

"Clammy and slick?"

"Yes!" she cried again, and clapped with delight. "You *are* the smartest boy in school, aren't you?"

"At *this* school, there's hardly much competition," he muttered.

"Well, I think you're *the* most smart and clever boy *ever*!" She attempted a winsome fluttering of her eyelashes. "*And* the handsomest."

He seemed not to know at all what to make of that, and certainly didn't rally back with a compliment for her beauty. Boys were *so* hopeless sometimes, honestly they were. Not that grown men were much different; Sarah often witnessed her own father needing pointed prompts to remark on Mother's new dress or hair style.

Before Herbert could decide what – if anything – to say, a giggling whirlwind of girls rushed to surround them. Not only her friends, but the younger girls from Mrs. Daunley's class – the ones who'd been jumping-rope while singing the cat song – and a few of the older ones as well.

Mary, of course, led the chant. "Herbie and Sarah, sittin' in a tree --"

"K-I-S-S-I-N-G!" the rest joined in.

"Stop!" squealed Sarah, giggling herself. And, she suspected, blushing her own shade of hothouse pink.

"First comes love," the girls chanted on, undaunted, "then comes marriage ... then comes Herbie with the baby carriage!"

"I prefer," he repeated, "to be addressed as Herbert."

The other boys, distracted from their game, had turned to look. Among them was Sebastian Crewe, who'd made no secret of fancying Sarah, while she in turn made no secret of *not* fancying him. Seeing her there with Herbert West, as the silly-chanting girls capered, he glowered. He threw down the ball with such a hard bounce that it soared over Tommy's head and rolled all the way to the schoolyard fence. Sebastian stomped after it with his face like a thundercloud.

At the main door, Miss Phelps rang the bell. Everyone began dispersing, gathering their things, getting ready to go back in. Herbert got to his feet, clutching his medical book.

"May I sit and talk with you again at recess tomorrow?" she asked, also rising, demurely brushing grass from her skirt.

He shrugged in a fitful, fidgety manner. "I suppose." His gaze strayed impatiently toward the school, where some of their classmates were already headed up the steps.

"Herbert?"

He looked at her, light blue eyes quizzical through his spectacles.

"You could, you know," she said. "If you like."

"Could what?"

She clasped her hands at the small of her back, bent forward, lifted her chin, and puckered her lips. Closed her eyes, too ... mostly ... peeking the teensiest bit to see his reaction ...

Recoiling with a look of alarm was *not* what she'd been hoping for.

"The bell," Herbert said. "Mr. Pym doesn't approve of tardiness."

With that, he was off, not at a run, but at a pace almost brisk enough to be insulting. Sarah blew out a breath in an exasperated sigh.

Boys. They honestly *were* hopeless, weren't they?

Sarah could hardly wait until recess the next day. It was difficult going, too, what with a packet of licorice candy in her possession. But if she so much as ate one piece, the other girls would see and want to share, and she had to save them for later.

"You oughtn't go about with him," Sebastian Crewe told her at lunch-time, lagging behind the other boys while the girls helped clean up. "With West. He's peculiar."

"I think he's nice," said Sarah.

"Peculiar," Sebastian insisted. "Too smart for his own good, that's what Mr. Pym says. Always going on about dead things and brains and such. He told our whole class that if you stuck a wire into a frog's head, you could make it kick its legs."

"Eew."

"Eew's right, and that's not the half of it! So, you oughtn't go about with him."

"Who I go about with or not isn't your concern."

"Sure it is. You're my girl."

"Says who and since when?"

"Everyone knows!"

"I didn't!"

"Well, now you do."

"Fancy that!" Sarah cried, flinging her hands in the air. "You don't get to be telling me whose girl I am!"

"I only meant --"

Miss Phelps came in then, ending the conversation with a stern look that sent Sebastian hurrying on his way as Sarah busied herself dutifully with cleaning.

The nerve of him ... saying she was *his* girl, telling her who she could talk to! Hmf!

When the recess bell finally rang, Sarah made no secret of her destination. She went bold-as-brass right over to the oak tree, and sat there with the packet of candies in her lap, waiting for Herbert West.

He arrived a bit late, clothes rumpled and spectacles askew, a cigar box tucked under one arm.

"What happened to you?" Sarah asked, though she already half had an idea, as if she couldn't guess.

"Nothing. Someone bumped me in the hallway, almost knocked me down."

"Sebastian?"

Herbert sat on the shady grass, straightening his spectacles. "He swears it was an accident."

"Oh, yes."

"But he also tried to trip me, so pardon me if I have my doubts."

"Herbert, I'm so sorry."

"Why? You weren't there. The other boys often pull pranks. They don't like that I'm good at lessons, and they make fun of me for living with my aunts."

She decided there was no need to explain. Why waste their recess on that? Besides, she noticed the cigar box and couldn't help but wonder what was in it. She'd brought licorice candies, after all ... perhaps he'd brought cookies or toffees or some other sweets.

"No book today?" she inquired, twirling her ringlet.

"I didn't want to leave this in my desk."

"What's in it?" She started to reach for the lid and Herbert drew the box toward his knee.

"Mice," he said.

"Mice?" Sarah snatched her hand back. "Why do you have mice in a box?"

"Aunt Gertrude keeps them as pets. Aunt Ludmilla keeps budgies, but the mice are better. Not as good as rabbits, but, better."

"*Mice?*" she said again.

"Not ordinary mice," he said. "Not common field mice. These are fancy mice. They're becoming quite popular in London. Aunt Gertrude has a friend there, Mr. Maxey, who raises them. Breeds them."

"May I see?"

"I don't think you want to."

"Herbert West, I am not some kind of silly, skittish girl who cries *eek* at the sight of a mouse!"

"Well --"

"Show me!"

He sighed and opened the box. Sarah steeled herself to look. She wasn't sure how a 'fancy' mouse might differ from the ordinary kind, but –

But she certainly had never seen mice like these before. Not ... not tacked out on a board with all four little pink paws pinned and the furry belly sliced open ... not bobbing in a jam-jar of murky liquid with the top of the head missing ...

That the mice were also, in fact, fluffy and cream-colored with pretty markings ... was rather of far secondary importance.

"They're *dead*," she said.

"Of course. I brought them to show the class, for my report on biological studies."

"Why are they cut up that way?"

"I'm interested in the mechanics of life. It is my belief and theory that, somewhere, perhaps in the brain or central nervous system, is the key to what animates us, what makes us live. And that if those secrets can be unlocked, we'll have mastered the mystery of immortality."

She gazed at him with admiration as he made this fervent speech, the most she'd ever heard him say at once, and by far the most impassioned. His light blue eyes fair to shone with excitement.

He, however, must have mistaken her expression for confusion, because he sagged somewhat. "You wouldn't understand."

"No, I do. You want to bring them back to life. Like my cousin's goldie-fishies, or the cat in the song."

"What?"

"My cousin," said Sarah, lowering the lid to conceal the sad sight of the splayed-open mouse, "has a goldie-fishie that she keeps in a bowl on her dresser. One day, she found it there ... you know ... floating. She was terribly sad, cried and cried. So, her father, my uncle, told her to say extra prayers that night at bedtime, and perhaps God would bring it back. When she woke in the morning, there the fishie was, swimming around, good as new."

Herbert tucked down the corner of his mouth in a rather dubious sort of way.

"It's true!" she said. "My cousin says it's exactly the same as ever, except for one white spot just on its head, where the angels kissed it alive again."

He removed his spectacles long enough to rub his closed eyes and pinch the bridge of his nose, the way Sarah's mother did when she had one of her headaches. "And the cat?"

"In that new song. The little girls were singing it just yesterday while they jumped rope."

"I wasn't listening."

"It's about a man who can't get rid of his cat. No matter what he does, the cat keeps coming back. He sends it away on a boat, and the boat sinks but the cat comes back. Then he tries a train, but the train goes off the rails and the cat comes back. He even tries dynamite."

"That's absurd," said Herbert.

"That's how the song goes." She cleared her throat, daintily, and sang. "Ole Mr. Johnson had troubles of his own ... he had a yellow cat that wouldn't leave his home ... he tried and he tried to give the cat away ... but the cat came back the very next day! Yes, the cat came back ... they thought he was a goner but ... the cat came back ... he just wouldn't stay away!"

"No, I meant, I believe you that's how the song goes," he said. "But you can't think it's true."

"Why not? Cats *do* have nine lives, after all." She giggled.

"If *you're* going to tease and make fun of me, too --"

"I'm not, honestly!" She held out the paper packet. "Would you like a licorice candy?"

He studied her a moment longer, wary, then relented just when she thought he was going to pick up his cigar box and go. "Yes, please."

So they sat, and shared the candies. She did most of the talking, not quite chattering like a magpie. It did not escape her attention that Sebastian glared at them throughout the rest of recess.

Nor did it escape her attention that, after school, instead of taking his usual route home, Sebastian – with a furtive air – went by way of the winding lane through Owl's Green. Following Herbert West, whose aunties lived in a ramshackle old house on the other side.

Sarah caught up with them on the wooded hill above the creek. She heard them before she saw them, too ... or, rather, heard Sebastian.

"... *my* girl!"

There must have been some scuffling already; Herbert's shirt was untucked and his spectacles hung on crooked by an ear-piece. His eyes burned pale gas-flame blue with anger. Their book-satchels, and the box of dead mice, had been dropped on the path.

"I didn't *do* anything," Herbert said, smacking away the accusing finger Sebastian jabbed at his face. "Point that at me again, and I'll break it, see if I don't."

"I'd like to see you try --"

"Sebastian!" she cried, rushing toward the boys. "Stop it!"

"Go away, Sarah!"

"I said, stop it! Leave him be!"

She hadn't known she could push so hard.

Sebastian yelled, arms pinwheeling, as he stumbled backward. Chunks of dark, crumbly soil gave way under his heels. Roots tore like little threads. Herbert grabbed for him, but missed. And Sebastian plunged over the edge.

He landed headfirst on the rocks, with an awful crunching thud. His body went all loose, flopping into the mud and muck.

"Ooh, we'll be in trouble!" fretted Sarah as she and Herbert scrambled down the embankment. "Is he dead? Do you think he's dead?"

"He must be, after such a fall."

"Well, *do* something!"

"Me? You're the one who pushed him."

"*You're* the one who's supposed to be such an excellent candidate for early admission to medical school at Miskatonic University!"

He blinked, then puffed up a bit, as if impressed she remembered. What a time for him to not be quite so hopeless after all!

They reached the bottom without falling themselves. The creek was low. Sebastian sprawled faceup on the bank, feet in the mud, a hand in the rippling water, surrounded by the loose earth he'd taken down with him

One eye was shut, the other open with the white part gone reddish. Darker red trickles ran from his nose and mouth. Herbert crouched over him, first pressing his fingers to Sebastian's neck, then bending to set his ear to the other boy's chest.

Sarah felt sick, as if she were going to vomit up her lunch – not to mention all those licorice candies. Or as if she might faint, the way ladies did, with a gasp and lifting her wrist to her brow.

Yet, she also felt strangely curious, interested. Distant from everything, somehow, the way she felt about stories in the newspaper that took place far away, but were still exciting to read.

It *was* Sebastian there, Sebastian Crewe; she knew it was.

Or was it?

His face didn't look the same. Parts of it looked lumpy, pushed out of place. And his eyes, of course, his eyes definitely didn't look the same. His body lay limp, disjointed.

The longer she stared at him, the more it really did begin to seem it wasn't Sebastian at all. More as if someone had made a fairly cunning likeness, a scarecrow or boy-sized rag doll, and dressed it in Sebastian's clothes and a wig.

But it *was* Sebastian, it was!

Wasn't it?

"If he is," she said, "if he's dead, I mean, you can fix it, can't you? You can bring him back. Like the cat in the song, and my cousin's goldie-fishie. Or, wait, I know! The headmaster!"

"What *are* you yammering about?"

"That flask he keeps in his coat! The revivifying, he calls it. We asked Miss Phelps once and she said it means something to liven a person up ... then she whispered something to Mrs. Daunley about how the old goat hardly needed it. But it might help, mightn't it? If we could get Sebastian to drink some?"

Herbert gave her an impatient, scornful look. "It's only gin, or whiskey, in that flask. You'd need something far stronger and more chemically complex to ..." He trailed off, his expression becoming thoughtful. "... hmm, though I do wonder ..."

"Never mind it, then!" said Sarah. "What about Sebastian?"

"His skull's fractured in several places," Herbert said, probing at the hairy, bloody mess that was the back of Sebastian's head. "The dura is torn ... look ... you can even see his brain ..."

Sarah wrung her hands. "Is he going to be all right?"

Fascinated, Herbert ignored her question. He took a slim wooden pencil from his pocket and poked around with it. He wiggled the pencil. He twisted it like a corkscrew, working it deeper. It made ghastly scraping and squishing noises.

Suddenly, Sebastian's arms and legs jerked, wild spasmodic jerks, like a puppet with tangled strings.

"He moved!" Sarah squealed, skittering a step back.

"Reflex," said Herbert, almost absently, wiping his fingers on his shirt to take a better grip on the pencil. "Involuntary. Nerve impulses responding to stimulation of the motor cortex --"

"Yes, fine. But it's helping! He's moving! Do it again!"

"All right." He turned Sebastian's head to the side.

Sarah tried not to grimace at the sounds of the pencil digging around in the broken skull. It grated against bone, which was bad. And squelched in brains, which was worse. The juicy squelching reminded her of Sunday suppers as her father carved a nice fat roasted chicken.

Sebastian's whole body bucked and lurched. His back arched up from the ground. His hands beat the air, as if swatting invisible flies. His left leg drummed madly, the way a dog's might during a vigorous rib-scratching. He thumped down again with a gurgling groan.

"You did it!" Sarah cried. She hopped up and down, clapping. "Whew, and good thing, too. I thought he was a goner!"

"Oh, he is." Herbert prodded some more. A strange, cold grin curved his lips as he watched Sebastian's fingers twitch.

"But, he moved," she said.

"That was me," Herbert said. "Manipulating the pencil within his brain triggers muscle movement."

"You did that? You made his legs move and his fingers twitch?"

"Yes."

She clapped again. "What else can you make him do?"

Herbert sat back on his heels and looked at her then, a long and rather odd look. Not the warm and admiring kind of look a girl might hope for from a boy, but a cool, evaluating one. He absently pushed his spectacles further up his nose as he did so, leaving a reddish mark on his fair skin, and the smudge of a thumbprint on one glass lens.

"What else can I make him do?" he repeated, askance.

Sarah nodded vigorously. "Can you make him sit up? Walk? Talk? Do a funny dance?"

"A funny dance? You do realize, he's dead."

"Are you sure?"

"Fairly."

"We killed him?"

"*You* killed him. You pushed him off."

"Well, *you* stuck a pencil in his brains."

"Only after the fall broke his skull."

"You still did. Besides, how can he be dead if he's moving?"

"I *told* you," Herbert said, with an impatient sigh.

"The pencil, nerves, motor cortex, fine-fine-fine-yes." She flapped her hand. "But if you can make him move, make him walk, then it's all right."

"Just *how,* exactly, is it all right?"

"We won't get in trouble. No one will have to know."

"His skull's smashed open."

"Then he can wear a cap! Honestly, Herbert West! Now, stand him up. Can you, or *can't* you?"

He set his jaw, showing that his pride had been stung. "Perhaps."

"Then get on with it." Sarah stepped daintily around to the other side of Sebastian and leaned over to peer into his lumpy, distorted face.

Funny, she no longer felt sick in the slightest. A momentary qualm from the licorice candies, no doubt. After all, while this *was* Sebastian, it really wasn't, was it? Not the Sebastian Crewe she'd known since forever, lively and bothersome.

His open eye, the one that had gone bloodshot, gazed past her, toward the treetops, with a blank, empty stare. She wondered, if she shined a light and peered very close into his dilated pupil, she might see the pencil's tip working around back there.

"This makes the fingers twitch ..." Herbert murmured as he fiddled and poked. "And this, the legs ..."

"Stand him up," Sarah urged. "What about his eye, can you open his other eye? He can't go home, or around town, with one eye shut. Someone will notice."

"I'm trying. And don't you think they'll notice if I'm walking behind him every step, wiggling a pencil in the back of his head?"

"Don't be silly."

Herbert hissed a breath through his teeth. He seemed on the verge of carrying on the argument, but at that moment a muffled sound like the crackle of gristle came from deep inside Sebastian's head and the pencil sank in another half-inch.

Sebastian's whole body lurched. The shut eyelid flew wide open – though that eye was, itself, canted off at an angle not the same as the other. His chest and stomach heaved. A choked, gurgling noise burst from his throat.

"Hhchhgluurk!" said Sebastian, or something like that.

His right arm flung suddenly upward in a clumsy arc. The back of his hand smacked Sarah on the hip, then slid down her leg, leaving a muddy blotch. His hooked fingers snag-tangled at her skirt.

She yelped, skipping back, snatching her skirt from his grip. His hand landed on her shoe. With another yelp, she kicked it away. It plopped into the creek again with a splash.

Sarah turned to Herbert, whose whole face was alight with excitement.

"Did you see --?" he began.

"That wasn't funny!" she cut in.

"What? But ... you told me to ..."

"Not to make him grab me. How rude!"

"I didn't *try* to make him grab you. It was involuntary, like I said."

"Well, it wasn't funny!"

His lips quirked, as if holding back a smile. It brought out a dimple, just one hidden lopsided dimple, on his cheek. If she truly *had* been very cross with him, she couldn't have stayed that way long. Not confronted with such an adorable dimple.

Doing her best to look cross, nonetheless, she folded her arms with a huff, the way she'd often seen her mother do.

"But didn't you see?" cried Herbert, half in frustration, half in delighted exuberance. "He moved, he even vocalized!"

"Hmf," said Sarah.

Finally, he said, "Fine, fine; I'm sorry," in the by-rote tone they all used when lectured by a teacher. Then a devilish kind of sparkle lit his pale blue eyes. "And he's sorry, too. Tell Sarah you're sorry, Sebastian." He gave the pencil another corkscrew twist.

Instead, Sebastian's whole body lunged up from the ground. "Ggllyaaachhk!" He tottered in an unsteady, staggering circle. His arms waved. His fingers jerked in spasmodic, clutching fists.

"Yes! Look at him! He's up! That's independent, volitional motion! Not mere reflex!" Herbert nearly danced with glee, and Sarah thought that surely he *must*, in the spirit of exuberance, kiss her *now*.

She did the prim-and-pretty forward lean again, but all Herbert did was continue to babble about the motor cortex, staring at Sebastian, lurching back and forth.

Then Sebastian made a blundering, but decisive, grab for Herbert. "Grahhhh!"

Herbert ducked away from the groping hands, uttering a yelp that sounded more excited than scared. "Did you see? He's attacking me!"

"He's trying to kill you!"

"Acting entirely on his own!"

"Sebastian!" Sarah shouted. "Stop it!"

Sebastian did not stop it. His ankles knocked together stupidly as he stumbled toward Herbert. Awful noises, grunting and groaning and gobbling noises, spewed from his mouth. So did bubbles of slobbering drool. It was quite, quite disgusting.

"Herbert, make him quit!"

"... doesn't seem able to speak, but ..."

A moment later, neither was Herbert, because Sebastian had him by the neck.

"Oh, honestly!" Sarah dashed up behind Sebastian and drove the heel of her hand hard against the end of the pencil, where it jutted out from his blood-matted dark hair.

The sensation of it was indescribably horrid, a sinking gelatinous but chunky squish, like sticking the handle of a wooden spoon into a mound of cold veal scraps encased in aspic jelly. Sebastian stiffened up on his tip-toes, quivering all over, and pitched headlong to collapse bonelessly face-down in the mud. Then he stopped moving altogether.

"Herbert? Are you all right?"

"What --" He coughed, rubbing his throat. "What did you *do*?"

"He was hurting you. I stopped him."

"You killed him."

"You said he was already a goner."

"Yes, but ..." Herbert knelt beside Sebastian, lifted a limp arm by the wrist, and let it drop. He heaved a sigh.

It was hardly the note of thanks she'd expected. She waited. She tapped her foot a little. But Herbert just kept peering and poking.

"Well, you're welcome," Sarah finally said, letting a sharp little hint of indignation show.

"Hm?" Adjusting his spectacles, he glanced up, as if surprised to see her still standing there.

"I saved your life!"

"Oh. Mm-hmm." He pinched the end of the pencil and wiggled it. The only response was a thick dribble from the hole in the back of Sebastian's head. "Hand me that stick, would you?"

She bent and picked up a stick by her shoe. "This one?"

"Yes. And that rock ... no, the other, the flat one with the edge ..."

"Why?"

"I need to open his skull if I'm to get a better look at his brain. Once I pry up this piece, here ..."

"But he's dead."

"I know." That avid, excited sparkle had returned to his pale blue eyes. "He's dead, now. He was dead before. But, for a while in between, he wasn't. All I have to do is figure out *how*."

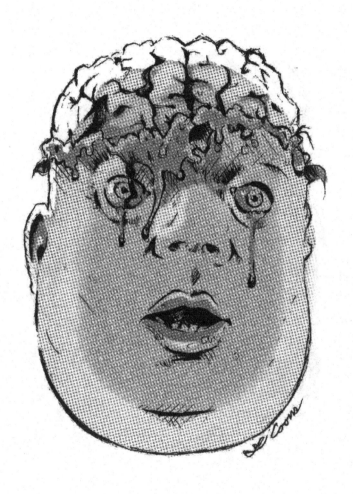

For more excellent work from Christine Morgan, check out her Splatter Western *THE NIGHT SILVER RIVER RUN RED*, or *AND HELL FOLLOWED* and *DIG TWO GRAVES Vol. 1*, two terrifying anthologies brought to you by Death's Head Press!